## DOUBLE ACTION

Morgan tried to roll away. A dozen boots thudded into him. One glanced off his face down across his eye. He could feel a flap of skin hanging down. Twenty, thirty times they kicked him.

"Enough," the first voice he had heard called softly and the punishment stopped.

"Bastard, you come to the wrong town. You picked the wrong boss. Tough luck. That's the way we work up here in the high country. This is your official welcome to hell, 'cause that's sure as hell where you're going to be in about ten seconds!"

Also in the *Buckskin* Series:

**BUCKSKIN #27**

# DOUBLE ACTION

# KIT DALTON

LEISURE BOOKS  NEW YORK CITY

A LEISURE BOOK®

June 2005

Published by

Dorchester Publishing Co., Inc.
200 Madison Avenue
New York, NY 10016

ISBN 0-8439-2845-X

The name "Leisure Books" and the stylized "L" with design are trademarks of Dorchester Publishing Co., Inc.

Printed in the United States of America.

Visit us on the web at www.dorchesterpub.com.

# DOUBLE ACTION

# Chapter One

Two .45 slugs snarled over Lee Morgan's head and another one plowed an inch furrow out of the edge of the building he crouched behind. The man lifted up, sent an answering round past the weathered, inch-thick shiplap, and tried to decide on his next move. He was getting low on rounds.

A light rain fell through the darkness and he wiped the drips out of his eyes. At the far side of the street, he saw two black shadows leave the protection of a farm wagon and dart past the rig's two harnessed horses and into the livery stable.

Damnit! That made six of them. Where did they all come from? How could he fight a whole damn army? Retreat, run away, live to fight another day? He looked behind him and saw the flash of a six-gun at the same time he heard the round go off. He dropped to his stomach in the mud and felt the slug jolt through the air just over his head. His hat went sailing to one side.

He looked to the left and bolted in that direction. He had no other option. Two men stood in the street blocking his path. He saw the long gun in one man's hand, a shotgun probably. Morgan fired two shots and the man with the scattergun swore and slumped to one side.

A round from the other man caught Lee in the right calf and knocked him down. He blasted twice more with his six gun at the dark shadows ahead of him, then the hammer came down on already spent cartridges.

A man laughed in the blackness.

"Well, well, well. Look what happened to the big man. He done run out of rounds."

"Fun time?" a new voice asked from in back of him.

"Why the hell not, for now," the first voice answered.

Morgan grabbed the barrel of the empty gun, felt the comforting warmth from the twenty rounds he had pumped through it, and now held it like a club.

Somebody kicked him in the thigh and it jolted him to the left. Another shadow from that direction thrust a rifle barrel at him, jabbing him in the belly, almost causing him to vomit.

A new voice called to him from ahead in the rainy darkness. Before he could spin away from danger, someone clubbed him with a six-gun from behind. Morgan knew he was going down.

*Never go down in a brawl or you're as good as dead.* He remembered that advice, had used it more than once himself.

When he hit, he rolled to the side and swung his six-gun at the closest shadow. He caught the man on the shin and sent him limping away howling in pain.

Then they moved in closer. Out of the wet darkness, a kick jolted into his side. He spun around on his knees and caught a boot in his belly slamming him over on his back. Then a knife flashed in the faint light from the livery stable lantern, and he felt the searing red agony as the raw steel cut through living flesh on his arm.

He tried to cover up his head. *Protect your head and balls*, was the other advice freely given for a brawl. His hands clasped the back of his head and his arms curved over his face as he brought up his knees to form a ball.

A boot jolted into his shot right leg and he bellowed in pain.

"Damn, he's still alive!" a voice shrilled.

A heavy shoe drove past his arms and slammed into the side of his head. It blurred his vision, his head felt light. Bile surged in his throat and he swallowed it down.

Then a heavy boot hit the other side of his head lifting him up and rolling him over. This time he saw stars and rainbows and all kinds of colored lights before a black cloud came dropping down, only to lift at once.

He tried to roll away. A dozen boots thudded into him. One glanced off his face down across his eye. He could feel a flap of skin hanging down. Twenty, thirty times they kicked him.

"Enough," the first voice he had heard called softly and the punishment stopped.

"Bastard, you come to the wrong town. You picked the wrong boss. Tough luck. That's the way we work up here in the high country. This is your official welcome to hell, cause that's sure as hell where you're going in about ten seconds!"

The sound of the cocking weapon caught Morgan's attention through his foggy mind. Dully, he heard the sharp report of a shot followed immediately by a tremendous pain in the middle of his back. He had never experienced anything so agonizing. Then the blinding black cloud swept down on him again and there was no more hurt, only the blackness.

The six men stared at the body sprawled in the mud and rain on the side of the street.

"He dead? Maybe we should check," one voice said.

The first voice rejected the idea. "Hell, no. I know where I shot him—the bastard is halfway to hell already. Now, one at a time we show up at the saloon, right? Not a word about this. We just got into town."

The voices faded as the men walked up the street.

The rain intensified and the body that lay in the middle of the street just down from the livery stable soaked up the wetness. The body was stretched out on its stomach and the rain water slowly mixed with blood and ran off his back to the ground forming a light red pool.

Faith Davies huddled in the doorway of the closed hardware store half a block down. She had heard the shootout, seen some of the men, and had heard the voices and then the final shot. She cowered back in the shadows of the recessed doorway as the six men walked up the far side of the street on the boardwalk.

They were talking, laughing. One of them was taller than the others and she saw that he wore a high crowned white hat. She waited until they were a half block by before she moved. She had a small umbrella, and she wasn't afraid to get wet. Even though, she shivered. She was sure they had just killed that man up there.

When all six had passed, she hurried down the street to where the man lay. She bent over in the rain and her small hand reached toward the victim's throat and pressed at the side to find the artery that pumped blood to the head.

She could see the wound in his back through a light jacket. Anyone shot in the back there certainly should be dead.

A soft groan came from the body, and she felt a firm steady pulse. He was alive! Faith squatted there a moment huddled under the umbrella. She couldn't help him, he must weigh twice what she did.

Faith stood and aimed the umbrella forward and ran through the rain. She hurried with unladylike speed, but she didn't care. Her father's house was a block and a half away. Not many people out in the rain this time of night.

It was nearly ten minutes later that Faith Davies and her father, Dunc, hurried through the now heavy rain toward the wounded man. Dunc pushed a wheelbarrow. As soon as they got there, Dunc touched the man's throat, grunted, and had Faith hold the barrow steady. He draped the big body in the wheel rig. When the man was on board, Dunc rested a minute. He saw something glinting in the mud. When he reached down he found a six-gun.

"Damn, must have been under his body," Dunc said. "Must be his shooting piece. We'll take it along."

Then Dunc grabbed the handles and pushed his burden slowly down the muddy street.

The rain came down harder, soaking all three of them.

"Six men, Pa. Don't know who they was, but one was taller than the others. Had a kind of high voice and wore a tall white hat that I seen in the light at the saloon."

"Damnation, but he's heavy," Dunc growled through the strain of pushing the barrow through the mud. "At least this infernal rain will wash out our tracks in an hour. Just hope them jaspers don't come back and show the deputy where they seen this body."

"They said he was dead."

"Not hardly."

They continued down a block, then another half block to the alley and up to the back door of the second house. Dunc pushed the barrow right up to the two steps, then both of them dragged the man by his shoulders through the kitchen door and into the big room.

"Build up the fire, Pa, and put on some water to heat. I'll look at his hurt."

They lit a coal lamp and turned up the wick. Faith found some old washed and opened flour sacks, and gently lifted his jacket and shirt. She used a towel to dry him and gingerly looked at his wounded back. There was little blood there. She pushed a folded compress on the bullet wound and stared at the strange purple line around his back toward his chest.

She showed it to her father. "Whatever could have made that mark?"

"Damnation, look at that. Seen that onct in the big war. Bullet went in this guy's back, hit a rib and slanted along the rib trying to bust through the skin. Skin gets tough, so the slug kept going around just under the skin. Lead tore up the meat in there like a bad bruise and made the purple trail. Could be what happened here. Best turn him over."

Faith wiped up the blood on his back.

"Let's ease him over on his back," her father said.

When they pulled back his muddy shirt they found a small exit wound where the nearly spent round punctured the skin on his chest and came out. There was only a little blood to mark the spot.

"Be dadburned!" the man said. "Now that is a pistol. By rights this gent should be dead and gone."

The man looked up. "Faith, we better get him undressed and washed and into bed. Hard telling what
damage them boots did kicking him that way. Could
be busted up inside and his head hurt real bad. Look
at that flap of skin off his forehead."

Her father watched her a minute. "I better stay
here and help you. Boys down at the saloon have
to do without me on our regular Wednesday night
poker game."

Faith smiled. "You go on, Pa. You'd rather miss
supper than that poker game. Least we know now
that he ain't gonna be dying on us. First, though,
you help me carry him into my bed. I'll sleep on the
couch."

"Yep, I'll help do that. But I better stay here. He's
big and has that gun. No telling what he could do."

It took both of them heaving and struggling to get
the big man down the hall to the first bedroom.
Faith spread an old blanket over her bed, then they
lifted him onto it.

"Thanks, Pa. You run along now. Down there you
might hear some men bragging about a killing. See
what you can find out. I'd sure like to know who
those six men were. Anyway, it's been a long time
since I got to play nursemaid."

"You sure?"

"Yes, Pa. He's in no condition to be any threat.
I'll wipe off his six-gun and hold it if he gets mean.
But he won't. Anyway, he needs some care."

Faith peeled the man's shirt half off him, lifted
up one shoulder and snaked the dirty, wet cloth out,
then took it off his other arm. His broad chest
showed thick with brownish blond hair.

"He might not even be conscious for three or four
hours yet," Dunc said. "From what you said he took
some nasty licks from those guys' boots. Maybe I
will go down to the saloon, keep my ears open,

maybe hear something."

Dunc Davies put on his hat and an old slicker and opened the back door. "Stopped raining," he said. "I'll put the wheelbarrow away on my way."

Faith waved and then checked the water on the stove. Not hot yet. She wiped the bloody spot on his chest with a cold cloth. He reacted to the cold with a gentle stirring.

A few minutes later she had the hot water and soap and a wash cloth on a chair beside her bed. First she washed off the wound, then his arms and chest and his neck and face. He didn't react at all to the warm water. He was dirty and mud splattered even through his shirt. She dried him off as she went.

Faith hesitated as she looked at his muddy pants and his boots. It had to be done. She wasn't going to have all that mud and dirty mess in her clean bed.

She checked his boots, cowboy type, no laces. Gingerly, she wrapped an old towel around his boot and tried to take it off. It was a task. At last with a lot of pulling and tugging, she got both off. She set them aside to clean later.

Faith paused as her hand reached for his belt, then she shrugged, undid the belt and opened the buttons down the fly. She pulled and tugged again and at last his pants and his summer underwear came off at the same time. She put them with his shirt in a pile for washing.

She looked at his crotch, staring a moment, then she turned, blushing, feeling the heat on her neck and chest. She shook her head, rinsed out the wash cloth and busily began washing him from waist to toes. She finished scrubbing the mud and dirt off him, then rolled him over and washed his back. At last she pulled away the old blanket.

More pushing and rolling and she had him tucked

between her very own sheets. Faith found a roll of white tape and fixed a bandage tightly over both the wounds on his back and chest, then did the same thing to the one on his right calf. The wound in his leg was in two places where the bullet went in and out. She taped up the flap of skin over his eye. It wasn't as bad as it first seemed.

There wasn't anything else she could do for him. She took some of the flour sack strips and bound up his leg so it wouldn't bleed any more.

Then she kept the fire going in the kitchen and closed off her pa's bedroom and the living room so most of the heat would come into the bedroom.

Last she pushed the covers up over him to his chin and made sure his breathing was deep and regular.

Faith spent the rest of the evening watching the man in her bed and keeping the fire going. Usually, this time of night she'd let it go out. Somehow it seemed right to be sure he stayed warm. Once she lifted the covers and felt his chest with her hand. It was warm.

Back in the kitchen she saw by the clock that it was almost eleven o'clock. She'd bank the fire and let it burn out. Her Pa would be home soon.

Faith took the old magazine she was reading and went back into the bedroom. She moved the lamp over to the dresser and went back to leafing through the pages. From time to time she checked him but there was no change. He must be recuperating, his body working hard to repair the damage.

It was almost midnight when Dunc came in. He knocked the way he always did to let her know it was him, then he was inside and holding his hands over the fire.

"Raining again. How's your patient?"

"Still sleeping."

He nodded. "Good. From what I hear that tall man in the white hat you saw was probably Tim Pickering. He and five other gents were in at the Hard Rock Saloon celebrating. Seems they earned some extra money tonight."

"By killing a man?"

"Could be."

"You never play cards at the Hard Rock Saloon."

"Did tonight. Had a feeling one of the shooters might be Pickering. He's been pushing folks around in this town for more than a year now. He just about lives in that saloon."

"Good Lord! I hope he didn't know that you had anything . . . I mean, we certainly don't want him to be angry at us."

"Too late for that, now, girl. We'll just keep our mouths shut and see what happens. If we need to stand up to Pickering, by damn, we will!"

Faith smiled at her father's bravado and touched his arm. "At least we won't have to do that tonight. Our friend is resting well. I think I'll sit up in the rocking chair for a while and see if he needs anything."

Dunc Davies smiled. He was a little smaller than average at five-five. He had a pot belly from too much good food and too little exercise, since he was the only watchmaker and repair man in the small town. His black hair had some streaks of gray and he wore small round eyeglasses with golden rims. Now his usual smile slipped over his concern.

"Yes, you sit a while, Faith. But remember, we don't know a thing about him. He might be just as bad as Tim Pickering."

Dunc went out, and she heard him in his room for a while, then all was quiet.

She sat there in her room listening to the man's even breathing. She figured he must be at least six-feet and two-inches. His hair was blondish brown and he was clean shaven except for a day's growth of stubble.

He had several scars on his body where it was obvious that he had been wounded before by bullet and knife. But his face was gentle, with a strong mouth, square chin. He had a look of a man who knew exactly who he was, what he wanted from life, and had the power to get it.

Could he be a killer and outlaw like Tim Pickering? Not a chance. She watched him a minute more, then turned down the lamp and let the magazine fall in her lap as she dozed off.

Faith woke twice that night, and at last went to the couch in the living room where she spread out two blankets and slid between them, still dressed except for her shoes.

His head hurt like a hundred wild horses were stampeding across it. His chest and back sent urgent pain filled messages to his brain. His leg seemed to be on fire. At least he was warm and dry and in a bed. He decided all this before he opened his eyes. He had made no movement after he awoke. He had done that from long experience, but not because of any present problem or danger that he knew about.

He opened his eyes and saw that he was in a house, that it was daylight, and that an extremely pretty girl stared down at him. Before he wondered where he was, he watched the girl. She was short, slender, with an unruly and mostly uncombed mop of brown hair spilling below her shoulders and covering up half her face.

With a natural move, she brushed her hair out of her face and he saw light green eyes, a snub of a nose, high cheekbones with gentle hollows below and a small, soft mouth with pink lips that had just parted in surprise.

"Looks like you're awake," the girl said. "I'm Faith Davies and I live here."she grinned. "In fact, that's my bed. You were hurt. I found you and my father and I brought you here and helped you."

He looked at her and his grin slowly faded. He was about to introduce himself to this pretty lady, when with a shock that was like being shot, he realized that he didn't have the slightest idea what his name was, where he was, or why he might be in this community.

# Chapter Two

The man with two bullet holes in him and a slashed arm watched the woman carefully. "Miss Davies, I thank you for all you've done. Somebody did a good job trying to kill me. You probably saved my life. I can't tell you who I am or why I'm here, not yet. I hope that will be all right?"

She smiled a little tentatively. "Of course. Any time six men gang up on one and then shoot him when he's flat in the mud after he's been kicked twenty or thirty times, I sympathize." The strange look on her face vanished when a little girl smile shoved it aside.

"Now, are you hungry? How about breakfast? I can bring you eggs and quick-fry potatoes and onions, bacon, coffee, toast and jam. Hotcakes if you want them, too."

"Yes, I'm starved." He felt under the covers. "I . . . I don't seem to be wearing much. You have my clothes?"

"Just starting to wash them. Still raining out so I'll dry them in the house. Pa has a nightshirt if you want it." She laughed. "Why not relax and play the invalid for a while and get your breakfast served in bed?"

"Done," he said.

His mind whirled. What in hell was going on? Who was he? What was his name? He must be in this town, whatever and wherever it was, for some reason. That he had to find out first.

Somebody evidently tried to kill him. He felt the bandage on his chest and the pain. It was like one rib had been shattered into a dozen chunks.

Faith watched him, then told him about the wound in his back and chest.

"Pa said he saw something like that in the big war once. A real lucky shot. A quarter-of-an-inch either direction and it would have killed you."

He saw the bandage on his arm, and felt one on his forehead. "You must be a real nurse."

"Not really. I'm a school teacher and out of work. There aren't enough children here in Silverville to start a school. Maybe next year. I stay with my father. He's the watchmaker here in town."

She left then and he heard pots and pans in the kitchen. She was humming a little song he didn't recognize.

Fifteen minutes later she came back in with a tray and his breakfast. The plate held three eggs, a pile of grated and quick fried potatoes, six slices of bacon and three slices of toast, jam, coffee and an apple.

She watched him as he ate with a frankly appraising stare.

"Faith, I've just arrived in Silverville and I don't know much about the town. Can you give me some information about this place? What's going on, who runs things, what kind of law is in town?"

"Sure." She sat in the rocking chair and smiled. "This is Silverville, California. As you know, we're at about four-thousand feet altitude in the edge of the Sierra Nevada Mountains and this is gold and silver mining country. Silverville is a hanger-on after the major strikes. Most of it is worked out around here but we have two big silver mines that just keep going and going."

She got up and poured him another cup of coffee. "So that's about it. Maybe 500 people in town. Most everybody works at one of the big mines, the Silver Queen or the Big Strike Number One. We have a few stores, not many, and no school, one church, one hotel and seven saloons."

He went on eating. So why did he come to this little mountain town? Surely not to work in the mines. To work for one of the big miner bosses? He'd done that before. That thought stopped him. A bit of memory coming back. He'd worked for a mine owner before. Doing what?

". . . so Pa came here about four years ago and I came last year when they said they would open a school, but they didn't, and couldn't, so I just stayed on." She looked up with those pale green eyes. "More coffee? Another couple of eggs?"

"No, this is fine. More than I deserve. I was very hungry."

He wanted to ask about his horse. There might be something in the saddlebag or bedroll that would help him remember who he was. But she'd want to know what color horse he rode, what kind of saddle. He didn't know. Damn!

He pushed the tray away with the empty plate. "Thanks for the breakfast. One of the best meals I've ever eaten. I wasn't just hungry, I was starved."

She took the tray and came back.

"I'm not even sure who shot me last night. Did you see any of it?"

"Yes. I was frightened half to death. You came

around a corner and the other men were on both sides of you. There was quite a bit of shooting and then a man with a high voice laughed and said you were out of rounds. The six of them closed in and hit you and kicked you and stopped only when the tall man told them to. Then he shot you in the back and they went to the Hard Rock Saloon to celebrate. My Pa said he heard the six of them say something about they had earned some extra money."

"By killing me," the man said. "Great little town you have here."

"We're not all like that."

"I know, and I apologize. You saved my life last night." He watched her a moment. "Who do I thank for the bath?"

She laughed and blushed. "You were all muddy and dirty and bleeding and I wasn't going to put you in my bed like that. It was just part of the job of fixing your wounds."

"I appreciate it, especially the bath. I only wish I had been awake to savor it. Thanks for both the bath and the nursing. Now, what about my clothes?"

She jumped up. "Oh, I forgot, I have to wash them and get them dried. She looked down at him, the blush gone. "You just rest now, you need it. Let me see if you have a temperature." She stepped to the bed and put the back of her small hand against his forehead and let it stay there for a few moments.

"Goodness no, you don't have a fever. Good. I wouldn't know what to do for that. I do need to go over to Doc Johnson and get some ointment for those wounds."

"Clothes first?"

"Sure." She hurried out of the room. He grinned. She was as cute as a ladybug on a pink tulip.

He heard her singing softly in the kitchen. Good,

he thought, she was happy for the moment and he was probably safe from his assassins, whoever they were.

He was in a mining town in California. Why? Two big mines here. From time to time mines hired enforcers, gunmen. How did he know that? Had he hired out as a gunhand?

He saw his gunbelt and weapon hanging on a chair near the bed. With a long, painful stretch he reached the leather and brought it to the bed. It had been wiped clean and rubbed with neatsfoot oil. The watchmaker might have done it.

He took out the weapon. It had been dried off, cleaned and oiled. It was a Colt double action .45. Probably a model 1878 and had a six-inch barrel and checkered ivory grips. The metal was nickle finished. A six-gun. He furrowed his brows. How did he know the model number? He must know a lot about guns.

His hands seemed to know the weapon. He hefted it by the handle, lifted it, pretended to draw and aim. Yes, natural. It was his gun. Now just what the hell was he doing here?

She came in, saw the weapon and shivered.

"Guns still scare me. Always have. Is that loaded?" she motioned with her hand. "No, no it can't be, it wasn't last night. And there were six fired rounds in the cylinder."

"Six? That's a desperation move. I usually carry this piece with only five rounds because a jolt or bounce could make it go off if the hammer was over a live round."

"It was a desperate situation last night."

"Faith, did you clean and oil this weapon?"

"No, Pa must have done that. He appreciates a good watch, clock or well made gun."

"I'll talk to him. Now, is there a local newspaper?

That would be good background for me on the town."

"Sure, only four pages, but it comes out each week. I think I have a stack of them."

A moment later she left the room and came back with some papers all neatly folded.

"Last four weeks worth, will that help?"

"It will."

"Clothes all washed, now I'm drying them. Are you warm enough?"

"Yes, thanks."

He dug into the papers, reading every headline and each story that might give him some idea why he was there. He found a stabbing, two shootings, and the start of a murder trial, but nothing that might help him. There were stories about the mines in each issue, but again, not anything he could get a clue from. He put them aside.

"Any help?" she asked. There was a trace of moisture on her forehead. She wiped it away and still managed to look beautiful.

"Not much. Do you have any .45 rounds in the house? I feel undressed without a loaded firearm."

"You are undressed," she said with a grin. "I think Pa has some around."

She came back soon with a box of .45 rounds and he pushed out the six spent casings and filled the cylinder with five loaded rounds. He put the revolver under the pillow.

"Now that you feel safe from me, I'm going to leave you on your own for about half-an-hour while I walk over to Doc Johnson and get some salve for that cut."

He looked in his weather beaten wallet that lay on a small stand where she evidently had emptied his pants pockets. It held six dollar bills but no letters, cards or addresses. It had been a chance.

He took out two greenbacks and gave them to Faith.

"Buy two dollars worth if you can."

"He won't have a bottle that big." She took one of the bills and waved. "Don't go jumping around too much on that leg. It's going to hurt for a week."

Once she was outside, he sat up and began testing body parts. His left arm hurt like fire when he flexed it or lifted it. Easy with that one. He swung his legs out from under the blankets and looked at his right leg. Slug must have gone right through. That was good.

He frowned. How did he *know* what was good? Maybe he'd been a doctor. No. He put both feet on the floor and tried to stand. He screeched from the pain in his leg. He sat down on the bed and winced. A slow twist with his torso brought a dozen more pain reports from his back, his chest and all over his trunk. He looked down and saw the boot marks on his body that were slowly turning black and blue.

Again he tried to stand and this time made it with only a small groan. He saw a mirror on the dresser and moved toward it. He took two painful steps and held on to the dresser, then looked up to stare at a stranger's face.

No, not entirely a stranger. Somehow he knew there would be no beard, just two days' growth of whiskers. The blondish hair was a surprise. A face that could be hard, strong mouth, square chin, no sideburns. He pulled free the white tape over a small bandage and checked the skin over his eye. A boot must have scrubbed off some skin. A half-inch piece hung down on his eyebrow. Already his eye was turning black. There were some twitches and twinges in his brain. Something was coming back, but not fast enough, maybe not quick enough to keep him alive.

When Faith's Pa came home, he'd level with them and hope they could help him discover why he came to town. Then maybe there would be someone who hired him and he could dig out his name.

"Hired him," he said it out loud. He had used the term automatically. Was he a gun for hire? As soon as he could, he'd go out in the woods and shoot. He'd find out if he was good with a six-gun or not.

Someone knocked on a door somewhere. He listened again. Front door. He waited. The knock came again, then once more. At last whoever it was, left. Must be a friend. He doubted if the door was locked.

He looked at his naked body for a moment, then moved back to the bed. He was sure his clothes weren't dry yet.

Laying there in the bed, he tried to jam the pieces together into something that would make sense, but he simply didn't have enough parts yet. The rest of the day to rest, then in the morning he'd start solving this damned puzzle.

Faith woke him a half hour later when she touched his shoulder. "Hey there, you sleeping in my bed. You feeling better?"

"Almost human," he said, blinking awake in an instant. His hand had stabbed for the revolver under his pillow. That told him something.

"Don't shoot, I'm friendly," she said as his hand touched the weapon. "Told Doc that Pa got some scrapes and scratches and a cut on his arm, and he gave me a jar of ointment and salve. He said it was good for cuts and tears and even gunshots. Let me fix up your hurts, then we'll think about some lunch. If you're hungry at all."

She treated his six different wounds, lifting the covers up from his feet to treat his leg. When she was through she bandaged the leg again and his eye.

Faith replaced the slightly bloody bandages on his chest and back.

She put the doctoring things on the dresser and walked out of the room. When she came back in a few minutes later, Faith carried a round, galvanized washtub.

Faith didn't say a word. She set it down and went out of the room and came back with a bucket of water. She poured three buckets of hot water into the tub, then brought in one of cold water and turned to look at him.

Her face was tinged with traces of doubt and uncertainty, then they faded away and she smiled. "Pa won't be home until about six tonight."

"So you're giving me another bath?"

"Oh, no," she said and grinned. "It's time for my bath. I figure that fair is fair. I mean, I gave you a bath. I undressed you and all. It's only fair that . . . that . . . that you get to help give me a bath. Any objections?"

He laughed and grinned. "Hell, no! I might have got kicked in the head a couple of times, but I'm not dead and I'm not crazy!"

Faith sighed and laughed nervously. "Oh, good, that makes it ever so much easier."

She walked over to him. "I'd like you to help me undress."

He frowned slightly. "Are you teasing me?"

"I never tease. I'm not a complicated person. I see something that I like, I make every effort to get it. Now please, help me undress."

He unbuttoned the fasteners down the front of her dress to the waist. She lifted it off over her head and stood there in her chemise and white cotton drawers that came to her knees.

Faith smiled. "Does your arm hurt too much to help me get my chemise off?"

"What arm?" he said as he sat up and lifted the chemise over her head. Her breasts were modest sized, pointed with softly pink areolas and small pink nipples that even now were starting to grow.

She was slender and well formed and she watched him.

"You're not disappointed?"

"To see a beautiful lady half naked? Who could be disappointed. I'm delighted."

She stepped away from the bed, turned her back, opened buttons and squirmed out of the tight drawers that went down each leg to her knee. Then, naked, she turned slowly. "This is me, here I am."

She looked around, then grinned and looked at his crotch and up to his eyes. "I . . . I . . . I'm not used to doing this. But I want to."

She moved to the tub, tested the water and then stepped in and sat down facing him. She took a small cloth and soap and began to wash herself.

"If you want to come over here, you can wash me. It's only fair because I washed you."

Another small note of memory flashed through his brain. Yes, he had washed a girl in a tub before. He kicked out of the covers and stood naked beside the bed. A flash of pain daggered into his brain but he beat it down. He paused for a moment so she could see his body, then he walked toward her.

# Chapter Three

By the time Morgan reached the small bathtub and knelt beside it, his penis was erect and urging him on. Faith looked down at it and grinned.

"How nice, I see now that we're both excited."

She handed him the wash cloth, but he put it down, soaped his hands on the bar and then began to wash her chest and her breasts. She glanced up at him, her smile edging with desire.

"If I were a kitten I would be purring by now," she said softly.

He bent and kissed her lips. They were stiff at first, then warmed and pressed hard against his. His tongue flicked at her lips and they parted and he let her come into him first. Her tongue darted in, a flaming sword that seared him and made him forget all of his aches and bruises. Slowly their lips parted and he kissed her nose, then both her eyes.

"A woman is so marvelous, do you know that? All bristle and bluff one minute, then all heat and passion the next. You never know which woman is in her body at any time. I like them both, but I love the passionate one best."

His hands concentrated on her breasts and then she caught one hand and pushed it down below the water. She sat crosslegged in the tub and his hand caught at the swatch of floating brown fur. She shivered, then reached out and touched his erection.

"Yes," he said as he nibbled at her ear. "Play with him."

She sighed and washed off the soap from her breasts. She held his shoulder and got up on her knees.

"You forgot to wash one piece," she told him. Then her lips found his again and he reached down and soaped her crotch, now out of the water. He washed her thoroughly until one finger penetrated her soapy vagina and she gasped in surprise and pleasure. He washed off the soap and bent to kiss her wet breasts

Slowly he licked them off, then bit her nipples gently until she growled at him and began to stroke his penis.

"I . . . I . . . I think I've had enough of a bath," she said, her eyes shining as he'd not seen them do before. He caught up a soft, fluffy towel she had laid out and dried her hands and arms, then her chest and gently dried her breasts.

She grabbed the towel and dried her legs and back and then caught his hand and urged him to her bed. She lay on her side and watched him. He eased in beside her and kissed her available breast.

"Seduce me," she said so softly he barely heard her. He glanced up and she nodded.

"Have you made love with a man before?" he asked.

Her reply was faint and he had to strain to hear. "Once, when I was sixteen and he was fifteen. He barely penetrated me but he said it counted. I think he was keeping a running total. Please, seduce me slowly."

He did. When he got down to her breasts, he kissed them and petted them. She panted and smiled and urged him on, holding tightly to his penis all the time.

When he touched her clitoris twice she broke into a climax that he thought would never stop. For almost two minutes she raced from one pounding, shattering climax into the next, until she was so exhausted she lay beside him panting, her eyes closed as she gulped in air.

"Oh, lordy," she said. "Oh, lordy!"

When she had recovered she looked at him a long time, then slowly bent and kissed the purple tip of his penis.

"Oh, yes!" he said.

She looked up. "You like that?"

He nodded. She kissed it again, and again, then opened her mouth and pulled the purple head inside. Her tongue teased him and stroked him. Slowly he drew partway out, then eased back in. She picked it up and bounced up and down on him for a moment, then he pulled her head up and kissed her lips.

"A guy can stand only so much of that pleasuring," he said.

She grinned and he moved his hand back down to her thighs. At once they parted and her knees lifted.

For the past twenty minutes he hadn't felt a single hurt. What good medicine a little sex was!

He rolled toward her now and his lance touched her soft little belly. She looked at him, eyes wide. Slowly she began to nod.

"Yes, yes, please. Right now. I'm ready."

He moved between her legs and lowered and found she was wet and more than ready. He was surprised how easily he slipped into her, then her legs lifted from some primal urge and locked around his back. The two bodies rocked and plunged and crashed into each other like a pair of over-anxious cow ponies trying to pull as a team in harness.

Faith whooped and shrieked and then she climaxed again, and again. She was shuddering and vibrating and spasming so fast and repeatedly that he gave up counting. Slowly he built up his own feelings and he realized he had learned something else about himself. He was used to making love. He was not a quick shot artist. It took some time and that took some performances.

When he at last powered over the final obstacle and raced down the other side into his climax, it was so good he didn't see how it could ever be that good again. He shattered into a million pieces.

At last he rolled on his side to take his weight off her small frame. She began to cry at once. He quieted her and kissed away her tears.

"I always cry when I'm happy," she said at last. "Right now I'm so happy I can't think of ever being so happy again. It was pure heaven and I know that now every time I'll compare making love to this time, and it'll come up short."

He kissed her. "Don't compare, just enjoy it every time, get the most feeling and pleasure that you can. It's a part of living and one of the best parts."

They lay there in each other's arms for ten minutes more, then she stirred.

"Maybe I should get up and get dressed," she said.

"Why?" he asked.

She laughed, kissed his nose and snuggled in his arms again.

A half an hour later they at last sat up on the bed. "I'll get your clothes," she said. "They should be dry by now." She stood and ran to the door.

"Hey," he called. She stopped and turned, naked and glowing from making love. "I just wanted to see you that way. What a beautiful sight."

She grinned and hurried out, her round little bottom twitching until he couldn't see her any more.

By the time she had a fire going and was getting dinner ready, he had learned more about the town.

"We figure another two or three years at the most," Faith said. "Then the silver will be gone, and so will Silverville. There's nothing else here for a town to live on. This will all be just another ghost town in ten years. The cold winter winds will whine through this house, flapping the shutters, and it'll become a house for coyotes and a bear, or maybe just squirrels and rabbits, with some blue jays and hawks in the attic.

"The miners are used to it," she said. "Most of them are used to moving every year or two at the most. The exception is the Mother Lode over in Virginia City. But there's only one spot like that around."

Faith had stitched up the bullet hole and cut in his shirt. He felt downright comfortable in front of the cookstove, warming his hands over the hot metal sides. The rain had stopped again.

She looked at him. "Put on your gunbelt," she said. "I want to see how you do it."

He shrugged, got the gunbelt from the back of his chair and strapped it on, then he tied the rawhide thong low on his thigh to keep the holster from riding up when he drew.

"There!" she said. "The way you tie down your holster. A man once told me I could tell a fast gunman when I saw a holster tied low that way. He said it was so all of the movement of a fast draw went into the weapon coming out of the holster, not of the leather moving up even a hundredth of an inch. Are you a gunman?"

He looked at her. It was time. He shook his head. "Faith, I just don't know. I guess I've lost my memory. You said I got kicked in the head a few times. My brain must have gotten rattled around and I can't for the life of me remember what my name is, or why I came to this town. I didn't even know the name of the town or the state, until you told me."

She was at his side in a minute, her arms around him, her head against his chest. "Poor darling!" She leaned back. "No wonder you wouldn't give me your name. You didn't know it!"

"I also don't know why those six men tried to kill me. Not knowing that could get me killed for sure the next time and you right along with me."

"Don't worry about us. Pa said he heard some men talking last night in a saloon. We think the man who wore the tall white hat and had a kind of high voice, is Tim Pickering. He's a no-good who most people think is a hired gun for one of the mine owners.

"We can find out for sure," Faith said. "But what about you? You're well spoken, so you have some book learning. You know firearms, so you could be an outlaw, a fast gun or maybe a detective or a lawman, a federal marshall, maybe!"

He grinned and chuckled. "That lawman label makes me laugh. I don't know why, but my guess is I'm not a lawman."

"Lots of other reasons them six could have been after you," she said.

"Like what? I'm open to guesses," he said.

"A detective, a Pinkerton detective tracking down some no-good who came through here."

"This isn't exactly on the main line to anywhere, is it? I'd guess the road goes only in one direction out of town, downhill."

"Yeah, but still. . . ."

A knock sounded on the kitchen door. It was three knocks followed by a pause and then one more.

"That's Pa, he'll have some ideas." She ran to the door and unbolted it, then opened it.

The man who came in was short, with a pot belly, black hair and a big grin around gold frame spectacles.

"Well, you look a bit better now than when I saw you last," Dunc said as he took a quick inventory of his guest. He held out his hand. "Dunc Davies," he said. "I live here and this is a whelp of mine."

"Pa, don't ask him his name. Those kicks to the head made him lose his memory," Faith said.

Dunc tossed his hat toward a chair. "Memory gone? All of it?"

"Afraid so, Mr. Davies," Morgan said.

"Dunc, everybody calls me that." He squinted and twisted his mouth into a scowl. "Then you don't know *why* them varmints were trying to ventilate your hide last night in the rain?"

"Not the slightest idea, Dunc. I didn't know where I was when I woke up. I didn't even know what state I was in."

"Glory, glory, glory. We are in some kind of big trouble right here." Dunc looked at him. "Not a glimmer?"

"Straws. I knew I was using a double action Colt, little bits and pieces like that come to me now and then. Nothing to build on," Morgan said.

"We know one thing," Dunc said. "Tim Pickering is mad as a wet rattlesnake today. He expected somebody to find your body and get the deputy to haul it off last night. Kept waiting. Now he can't prove he killed you. I heard he took a quick trip up to the Silver Queen mine to report in to his boss, Sylvester Bibb. From what folks say, Pickering doesn't even go to the bathroom unless Bibb tells him to. When he gunned you down there was a reason, and an order from Mr. Bibb himself."

"Good," the taller man said. "All I have to do is ride out to the mine and ask Bibb what this is all about."

"You'd find out on the hot lead end of a couple of high powered rifles and be underground within ten minutes," Dunc said. "Not a good plan."

"I've got to do something. Maybe I should catch this Tim Pickering alone and have a heart to steel-bladed talk with him."

"Might work, but damn risky," Dunc said. "Let's ponder this. First, we do nothing tonight. Instead we think and plan and try to work out a good strategy."

"First, you have to stay out of sight," Faith said. "That means staying right here inside the house. Outside, one of them six could see you and I'd have to patch up more bullet holes. You've had about enough of those for a while."

"I can't stay here," Morgan said.

"Why not?" Dunc said. "Ain't the chow good enough?"

"It's fine, only . . . I'd be imposing on you and Faith."

"So I'll charge you rent," Faith said. "I've been wondering when you'd remember this." She went to a broom closet and lifted out a heavy cloth money belt. She carried it by one end and dropped it in the tall man's lap.

"What's this?" he asked.

"What's it look like?" Dunc asked. "A money belt that's been dried out some."

"It's yours," Faith said. "I took it off your wet body last night when I took off your shirt."

"What's in it?" the man with no name asked.

"I don't know. It wasn't mine so I haven't looked." She grinned. "I'm curious as a cat, though."

He opened the flap and reached inside. His hand came out with a sheaf of bills. Then another handful. He spread them on the table. They were twenties and fifties.

Dunc counted it. "Be damned. Over two thousand dollars here. That's more than I make in my shop in four years. You might not know who you are, but whoever you are, you're rich."

"Or maybe an outlaw," he said. "Any banks been robbed lately around this area?"

"Stop that, you're not a bank robber," Faith said. Her father looked at her.

"Yep, daughter, I'm thinking the same thing. A tied down gun and lots of money don't necessarily mean a bank robber."

"But it could," he persisted.

"Could just as well mean you're a rich man from St. Louis looking over your mining interests," Dunc said. "Now let's settle down here and figure out what's going on."

The tall man took a twenty dollar bill and gave it to Dunc. "This is for board and room. No arguments. And remember, I like lots of bacon and steak."

They all laughed.

He got up and began walking around the kitchen and living room. "Just exercising," he said. "I got to keep that leg working or I'll never walk again. I've been shot in the leg before.''

"Ha! You remembered something else," Faith said. "I don't much like the sound of it, but it's something." She ran into her bedroom and came back with a tablet and a pencil. "I'm writing down everything we know about you. You tell me what else you remember and maybe we can get your memory back without somebody else kicking you in the head.''

"Maybe," he said. "Maybe. But just in case, I'm going to sit in at the Hard Rock Saloon tonight for a beer or two, and see what I can hear or remember.''

"Not a good idea," Dunc said.

"You got a duster?" the tall man asked Dunc.

"Yep, be a mite short, but some folks like them short.''

"And an old slouch hat of some sort?"

"Yeah, I guess.''

"Good, I'll be going to the saloon tonight. If you're there, you don't know me, hear?''

"Damn poor idea," Dunc said and paused. "But if I was in your place, I'd do the same thing. We got to call you something. How about Harry?''

"Why not? I used to have an Uncle Harry." He stopped. "Write that down. We may get there yet.''

The meal that night was mashed potatoes and chicken gravy, fried chicken and green beans and corn on the cob. He ate until he nearly blew apart.

"Good supper," he said.

"Thanks, Harry. You going to help me with the dishes?''

He winced when she said the name, then remembered that was supposed to be him.

"Might as well, got time before the serious drinking starts down at the Hard Rock Saloon.''

# Chapter Four

After the dishes were done, Morgan, now called Harry, settled down to talk to Dunc. The older man knew this town inside out, and he might know something about a gunman being hired.

"Can I look at your side piece?" Dunc asked.

Morgan handed it to the older man who looked it over critically. "Nice piece. I used to deal in some firearms as a favor to a few good customers. No more. Now we've got a guy in town who's a real gunsmith, part time, but he's good at it." Dunc looked at Harry and tossed the weapon back to him. Morgan caught it, reversed it and slid it into the holster without a flicker or a wasted motion.

"Well now, neatly done." Dunc looked at Faith. "Write that down, too, the man is handy with a sixgun." He rubbed his chin, then blew his nose that had been dripping all day since his impromptu walk in the rain the night before.

"Just for fun, Harry, let's see you draw that weapon as if it was for real. Take on the kitchen stove over there, but don't shoot the poor thing."

Morgan had been itching to try a few draws

himself just to find out. He walked to the wall away from the stove and stood facing the iron heater.

"Now!" Dunc barked.

Morgan's hand had been hanging below his right thigh. Now it darted upward, caught the butt of the big .45, and started its upward trip out of leather. At the same time the handle came into his hand, his bottom three fingers closed around the grip and his first finger found the trigger guard and slipped into place.

As this went on, his right thumb caught the hammer and pulled it back cocking the weapon. The millisecond the muzzle cleared leather, his hand rammed the weapon forward bringing it up slightly in a perfect point-to-aim movement.

"Bang!" Dunc said. He looked at Morgan for a minute with his mouth open. Then shook his head. "Holy Christ! I've seen some gunmen in my years in mining camps. Never have I seen anything like that. No chance you learned to draw like that in some church pew, or even some lawman's office.

"You can draw, but can you shoot?" He walked around the table. "Hell, I got to know," Dunc said. "Come on out to the wood shed."

"You aiming to paddle him, Pa?" Faith asked.

"Yeah, and twice on Sunday. Final test for Harry. I'm gonna hold a stick of kindling, and call out, and Harry is gonna try to draw and hit the stick fast as he can. Want to try it, Harry?"

"Like you say, Dunc, we both got to know."

The woodshed was about twenty feet long from the edge of the inside kitchen door to the back wall. It was only half full of wood, it being July. They set up three lamps and a lantern down in the far end of the shed, and Dunc stood on the chopping block. He picked up a piece of one-by-four about a foot long and held it in his right hand.

"Better put on a glove," Morgan said. "Be easier on your hand just in case I do hit the wood."

They found a work glove and Dunc put it on.

"I'll hold the stick out arm's length. Don't shoot my hand off or I'll kill you myself. A watchmaker is damn useless with just one hand."

They both chuckled. Faith looked worried.

"Aim for an inch from the far end of the stick. I'll call out, 'now,' like I did before and you draw and fire."

Morgan took his stance, made sure that there was a round in the chamber next to the one under the hammer and nodded. "Ready."

Dunc looked at him and lifted the piece of wood. He held it steady at arm's length. "Now," he barked.

Again Morgan's right hand whipped up in a perfect draw, thumbed the hammer back, point-aimed and fired so quickly it was hard to see his hand.

The piece of wood jolted out of Dunc's hand and slammed against the wall behind him.

"Keeeeeerist in a bucket!" Dunc screeched. "I was trying to count how many seconds it would take you. I never even got off my one thousand, let alone 'and one.' Less than a second. I just never . . . never have seen nobody draw and shoot and hit anything that fast. Keeeeerist in a teacup!"

"That was one of your .45 rounds," Morgan said. "Maybe it wanted to do a good job for you." He rubbed his hand over his face. "All right, I guess that about finishes that part of the argument. I'm a gunman. Now all we have to figure out is if I'm on the side of the good guys or the bad ones."

Faith looked up quickly. "You could be somewhere in between."

Back in the kitchen, Morgan reloaded the spent casing and turned the cylinder so the hammer rested on the empty chamber.

They sat at the kitchen table. "I've got to go to the saloon and see what I can learn," Morgan said. "All I'm going to do is sit and have a beer and listen a little. I'm tired of not knowing who I am and what I'm supposed to be doing. Damn tired of it. I'll be needing that duster and old hat now."

Faith brought them.

"Stopped raining again," she said.

Dunc put on a jacket and his still wet hat. "I'll be having a beer or two as well. Different table. Hard Rock Saloon. Got to serve yourself from the barkeep. His name is Lewis."

They headed for the back door when Faith called.

"Hey, you two. I don't want either of you getting into any trouble down there." She held up the money belt with its $2,000 inside. "What do I do with this?"

"Hide it in the flour bin," Morgan said and she stuck her tongue out at him.

When Morgan entered the Hard Rock Saloon, he saw that it was one step up from a sawdust floor establishment. It was rough and temporary, but it had lasted six years. He took a mug of draft beer and paid his nickel. There was a table at the far end of the dimly lighted saloon and he sat there with his back to the wall. The place was only half filled.

A dozen miners were drinking, a few played poker, a couple gambled at the monte table. Nowhere did he see a tall man in a white hat.

Five minutes later Dunc came in, talked with the barkeep for a minute, rented a deck of cards for a dollar and set up a small poker game with two men he evidently knew. They used a table halfway between Morgan and the barkeep.

All Morgan could do was listen to voices. He

didn't hear any that he recognized from the night before. He went and bought another beer and thought of joining Dunc in the poker game, changed his mind and went back to the table.

He sat there another hour nursing the drink, then gave up and walked past Dunc's table.

"Any room for a new player?" he asked.

Dunc shook his head. "Not a chance, this is our last hand. Been playing together too long to let a stranger in." The other two nodded so Morgan walked out the front door and back toward the Davies' house. He took a detour down Main Street. Nothing looked familiar. The sheriff's office was on a side street and he could read the sign. The windows were dark but there might be someone there.

He gave up and headed back to the Davies' house. He could almost walk without pain now. There was the hint of a limp when he forgot himself, but with some willpower he could force himself to walk straight and even.

He knocked on the back door, three knocks, then two more.

"Harry?" the voice came through the door.

"Right," he said.

Faith unbolted the door and let him inside. She looked at him a minute, then walked up to him and held out her hands for his hat and the heavy duster. She put them in the coat closet then came back.

"Learn anything?"

"Not a thing."

"You don't like the name 'Harry,' do you?"

"Nope, hated that uncle, fact be known."

"I won't use it much."

She came close to him and reached up and kissed him. He kissed her back and put his arms around her, pulling her willing body close to him.

"I'm not a demanding woman, but anytime that you need some relaxation and Pa isn't around, I'll be more than pleased to help you release your tensions."

He put his hand on her breasts and caressed them gently.

"I appreciate that." He kissed her again, then let go of her. "I'm about stove in. I do need some more sleep. Tonight I'll be on that couch or the floor. You're back in that soft and warm bed of your own again."

"Yes, sir. First, let me check your dressings. I'll change them and put on new ointment and salve. Doc Johnson says it's the best healing combination he's ever seen."

A half hour later she had rebandaged him, and spread some blankets on the couch in the living room. He was asleep five minutes after he lay down.

She watched him for a few minutes, then found her magazine and read a little. Faith would wait up for her father.


When Morgan left the saloon, the trio did make it the last game, and then Dunc went out the front door with one of the players, Deputy Sheriff Telford Sanders.

"Look, Dunc. I open the office door and show you the papers, six or eight people might come in for some help. I just want to get home and to bed."

"Damnit, Telly, you promised me, that's why you got in the game with only two dollars. Now come on, a promise is a bond."

"Hell, all right. Don't see why you're so interested anyway. I'm the law here, not you."

"Keep telling you, the Sheriff over at the county

seat told me to watch out for jewel thieves selling stones. If I know who to watch for it's easier, that's all. Damn, Telly, what's another half hour?"

They went down to the Deputy Sheriff's small office with one cell in back and he lit a lamp and moved it to the inside office and closed the door. He opened a top drawer with a stack of wanted posters in it.

"Hell, Dunc, here they are. You look these over and lock the door when you leave and push the key back under the door. I got one myself. I'll see you tomorrow."

He left.

For the next hour, Dunc looked through the drawer full of wanted posters. He was almost at the bottom of the stack when he pulled one out that had a picture that was a remarkable likeness. Most of the pictures were fuzzy and hard to make out. This one was plain and true to life.

"Wanted for Murder. DEAD OR ALIVE. Lee Buckskin Morgan. Reward $2,000. Tombstone, Arizona Territory. For the shooting death of Wilfred Potts. Contact Tombstone Sheriff, Tombstone, Arizona Territory."

The picture was perfect right down to the slight squint of his eyes, the square jaw and tumbled blondish hair that covered the tops of his ears.

It was the same man. Lee Morgan was the name of the man in his house. The man with the quick gun and the poor memory. The man at home alone with Faith. He folded the wanted poster and put it inside his shirt, then slammed the drawer and hurried to the door. He fumbled with the lock, then he took a deep breath. He had to calm down.

There was no rush. Morgan was not the kind of man to take advantage of a woman . . . unless she wanted to be pleasured. Faith was a grown woman now, and what she did was up to her. Anyway, he'd learned a lot more about Morgan in talking with him tonight and watching him that the damn piece of paper said.

He'd heard of wanted posters being put out that really shouldn't go out. Too late to call them back then. They might sit around in drawers in sheriff offices for twenty years. Most of them were not dated. Lots of wanted posters were sour grapes over legal self defense shootings.

He wouldn't tell anyone about the poster, he decided. He'd see what developed. If somebody did hire Morgan to come into town as a paid gun, it probably would be Bibb. But if that was so, why would the mine owner tell his hatchet man, Tim Pickering, to gun down Morgan?

No, it had to be the other way. Maybe the other mine owner, Janish Lang, had sent for Morgan to try to even up the fire power from Pickering. Now there was an idea.

Dunc walked slower as he neared the house. He couldn't slip up and use Morgan's real name. Why not change the name they called him? He and Faith knew a relative named Buck. Buck Wilhouse, a cousin of hers in Michigan. He was a tall guy, too. Yeah, he'd give it a try in the morning.

Dunc had looked at Morgan's hands as he ate. He had no callouses, no rope burns. He was not a miner or a cowboy. If he were, his hands would show it. What did that leave? A gambler or a gunman.

When Dunc came in the door, Faith held up her hand to quiet him. Dunc saw Morgan sleeping on the couch. He had a drink of water, and found his nightshirt and crawled into bed. He had a mystery to solve. There was nothing Dunc Davies enjoyed more than a good mystery.

When morning came, Faith found Morgan was up before she was. He had a fire going and coffee boiling. She stared at him sleepy-eyed and realized she must look a fright. She hurried back into her room to wash her face and comb out her long brown hair so it billowed around her shoulders.

When she came back out, Harry and Dunc were talking over cups of coffee at the table.

Dunc looked up. "We just decided that Harry doesn't fit this young man. We're gonna call him Buck instead. He's tall like your cousin Buck, and should be easier for us to remember. He's agreed. So, goodby Harry, and hello Buck."

"What kind of orders do I have for breakfast?" Faith asked.

"Usual for me," Dunc said. "Stack of cakes and some hot syrup and a gallon of coffee."

"Nothing for me," Morgan said. "I'm off on a walk so I can make sure this leg works when I want it to. My left arm is a little tight too, but it should be healing. I'll be back in an hour or so."

Morgan finished his coffee, waved and put on the slouch hat that pulled down over his face and headed for the alley. The first stop he was going to make was the livery.

The six men had attacked him outside the livery. That should mean that he had already left his horse there. That was the only way to come into Silverville, by horse or stage. He doubted he came on a stage.

The morning was bright and cool for July. The sky was washed and bright, the green from the rains lush. He walked down two blocks, saw the livery at the end of the next block and got there just as the stable hand was cleaning out stalls. The kid was sixteen, and had red hair.

"Were you on when I brought my horse in two days ago?" he asked the young man.

"Dunno, which was your nag?"

"I rented her and I'm not sure. There was some shooting just after I left outside the livery here. You probably remember it. Shooting in the rain," Morgan said.

"Oh, yeah. Heard some guy got blasted, but nobody ever found a body. Couple of guys came around the next day thinking he might have crawled in here and died. But I told them he didn't. I'm the only one dying here. Yeah, I remember the roan. You rode her hard and gave me a dollar to walk her out and rub her down. Did it, too."

"Good. Where is she?"

"Down this way." The stable hand led him along a shed to the next one and a stall where a big roan stood. She had on a feed bag.

"Oats?" Buck asked.

"You said oats every morning, hay every night and gave me five dollars in advance. I'm using up your money." The horse was unsaddled.

"Where's the tack?"

The young man pointed to a shelf behind the horse. "Right there, saddle, saddlebags and blanket. Now I got work to do." The kid took off with the five tined pitchfork growling about all the shit he had to throw around in this job.

Buck grinned and went to the saddlebags. The first side was empty. The other side had a pair of socks, a small notebook stapled on the top, the kind just big enough to slip into a pocket. He put it in his pocket and felt around again. A slip of paper. He took it out but couldn't read the faint writing in the poor lighting. He put it with the notebook.

That was all the bags had. The saddle was standard western, no marks, no number, no hand made artisan's signature. Just another ten dollar saddle.

He went out and found the stable hand. He took a five dollar bill from his pocket and held it out.

"Two things. Take good care of that horse. Remember who it is if anyone asks if the owner has been in. Right now I want you to forget that you ever saw me or know who in hell owns that horseflesh. Agreed?"

"Yeah, no trouble on my part. Oats and hay just a quarter a day. You're paid up for eighteen more days on that first five dollar bill."

"Keep that five yourself. Remember, you never saw me."

Buck headed out of the livery by the back door, circled around along a little stream hard against the slope of the mountain and found a log in the sun. He sat down, watched the creek a minute, then dug out the notebook and the piece of paper. Maybe now he could make some sense out of this whole affair.

# Chapter Five

There was no hesitation on Morgan's part. He wanted to know who he was. He unfolded the piece of paper from his pocket and read it quickly.

It was a bill of sale for a horse, a roan mare, the one he must have ridden into town. The receipt was made out to "bearer" and was dated a week ago. No help. He couldn't remember ever seeing it before.

He turned the small notebook over in his hand. He couldn't remember it either. The mare certainly didn't start any memories flowing for him.

On the first page of the notebook there was one word. 'Silverville.' So evidently he had intended to come to this small mining town. He flipped the pages. Three blank pages later he found some more words that made little sense.

One phrase was, 'missing three weeks.' On the same page was the word, 'miner.' A third entry was 'Chinese.'

The rest of the notebook was blank. Dandy! Why wasn't he the kind of man who wrote down everything in detail? That would have been a big help. His name and address on the inside flap would have helped, too. It also would have been too easy. His luck hadn't been running that way lately.

He almost threw the little book away, then stuffed it in his pocket and went back toward the main part of town. Buck, they were calling him. Fine, a damn lot better than Harry. He wasn't sure why he didn't like the name. Now he wasn't certain that he even had an uncle named Harry.

As soon as he went in the back door of the Davies' home, he smelled the fresh bread. That reminded him of home when his mother had baked bread. He frowned. Yes, his mother, the little ranch out west in Idaho. He had been very young, three or four, then they told him his mother went away and wouldn't be coming back. Another small fragment. Idaho. Yeah, that did feel right, familiar.

Faith looked up. Brown hair framed her face and covered one eye. She blew it away with a gust of breath.

"Just in time. You like fresh baked bread before it gets cool?" she asked.

"Does a range bull like to get to the young heifers?"

She laughed. "I don't know, but I'd guess they do. I'll write that down." She sobered. "Right now I feel like one of those young heifers." He went to her and kissed her lips lightly, felt her push her breasts hard against his chest. Then he stepped away.

"Faith, you don't know anything about me. I'm a gunman, right? That's all we know so far. I might even be wanted somewhere. Let's just slow down a little."

She shook her head, light green eyes giving her away before she spoke. "I don't care! You can have killed the governor and I'd still love you. There, I said it." She hugged him tightly and pushed against him all the way down to her knees. He could feel the heat coming from her slender body.

Gently he unstrapped her arms from his back. "You said something about hot bread? My all time favorite. My mother used to bake when we lived in Idaho. You can write that down. I wasn't more than four when they told me she had gone away. Now I know that she must have died or left us."

"We're making progress!" She kissed his cheek. "One of these days it's all going to come back."

"God, I hope so." She cut a slice off a just baked loaf, and tried to keep it from crushing together. She did well. He spread just churned and salted butter over the steaming bread and watched it melt into the whiteness. Then he added fresh apple butter on the bread and leaned back savoring each bite.

"A man could go soft and easy around here, around you. I bet you know that."

"Counting on it so hard it hurts."

"No matter what happens, I never want to harm you. Remember that. You're a beautiful, special, marvelous little lady, and you always will be. No matter what happens to me, you remember that, live long with that thought."

"Don't. That kind of talk scares me." She caught his hand and held it so she would have some contact.

"Don't worry yet. I still don't know why I'm here. As soon as the Hard Rock Saloon opens, I'm going to be watching it. Bet there are a few chairs sitting outside stores along Main Street, right?"

Faith nodded.

"I'll use one and watch for our tall man, Tim

Pickering. One way or another I'll find out what's going on."

Tears brimmed Faith's eyes. "You be careful. You go and get yourself killed, I'll come and spit on your grave!"

"Nicest thing anybody's ever said to me that I can remember," Morgan said. This time he kissed her cheek. "Now, I hate to bother an important, busy person like you are, Faith. But could I have another slice of that fresh baked bread?"

Two hours later, Morgan settled into a tilted back chair against the Silverville Hardware store's front wall and pulled the slouch hat down over his forehead so he could see a slot from under the brim. He aimed the opening at the front door of the Hard Rock Saloon and waited.

Once he almost went to sleep in the lazy morning sun, but he roused as men began going into the drinking establishment. After sitting there for an hour, he hadn't seen the tall gent with the white hat.

Morgan got up, stretched and knew his leg was stiff. He walked halfway down the block and back to loosen it up. He didn't hurt quite so much this morning. Faith had changed his bandages and said his back was coming along nicely. The swelling along the purple mark tracing his rib was starting to go down. He could see some of the black and blue of the tissue was fading.

His left arm still hurt like fire when he moved it wrong. He was most concerned with his leg. Without two good legs a gunman was about as much use as tits on a boar. Thinking about the use of such a phrase stopped him. Now where did he come up with that? It was a farm term. Would he know farmers in Idaho? What part of Idaho? He had no idea. One more bit of information for his catalog of himself.

Back at the Hard Rock Saloon, Morgan turned in, scanned the place quickly but didn't find anyone tall and no one with a white hat. He got a nickel beer and slid into a chair at a small table with his back to the wall.

A sharp-eyed dandy with a bright vest and a deck of cards in his hand walked up and nodded. "Got time for a little game?"

"Not hardly. Ride on down the trail."

The gambler shrugged and walked to a table where two miners had just sat down. He got a game there.

Buck took out the small notebook and stared at the page with the three entries on it. The word miner was obvious enough. Or was it? Did he come here to pretend to be a miner? To go to work underground and unearth some kind of conspiracy of highgraders, or maybe a killer? Maybe.

But if you put all the words together you had "Chinese miner missing three weeks."

Who was worried about Chinese, especially Chinese miners? The railroad had brought in thousands of Chinese late in the Sixties to help push the Central Pacific through the Rocky Mountains.

After the railroad was built and completed in 1869 the Chinese stayed in the country, some of them moving back to San Francisco where they established a real Chinatown. Others drifted into different kinds of work. He had heard that some mines in the west used a lot of Chinese. But in the short time he had walked around Silverville, he hadn't seen a single Chinaman.

The old problem came back. He was a gunman. So who brought him to town? Who had hired him?

Sure, he could ride up to each mine and ask the

owner if he was waiting for him. But if he picked
the wrong one first, he was dead and buried and
Faith was spitting on his grave.

Six men came in the door. They seemed to be
together, but none of them was anywhere near six
feet tall and none had on a white hat.

Morgan had another beer, got a deck of cards and
played some solitaire. Two hours later he decided
he never would win even one game of solitaire.

He was about to ditch the whole plan when he
looked up at two men coming through the door. One
wore a high crowned white hat, the kind that he'd
seen some Mexican *vaqueros* wear south of the
border.

He made a note to remember that. He'd been in
Mexico and knew about Mexican cowboys.

The man with the white hat got a beer from the
apron which he didn't pay for, swung his leg over
a chair back and sat down at a table. He started to
look around. Morgan concentrated on his beer and
shrugged a little lower in the chair.

The white hat gave up his visual search and talked
sternly to the other man he had come in with. It was
clear even from thirty feet away that the shorter
man was getting a lecture. Five minutes later the
shorter man went to the bar and brought back two
more draft beers. He pointed to the white hat and
didn't pay for them. The barkeep shrugged.

Morgan moved to see the man better and groaned
softly, his back was hurting more now. He had an
almost overwhelming urge to jump up, rush up to
Pickering and smash him in the mouth, knock him
over backwards, and then shoot the bastard dead
when he went for his gun.

Instead, Morgan finished off the mug of beer,
stood and went to watch a poker game at the table

next to the white hat. He heard the man's voice as he called to someone at the next table. Pickering's voice was high, a real tenor. He had to be the same man.

Morgan walked outside and sat in a different chair across the street by the barbershop. He could stand a haircut, but no time right now.

After about twenty minutes in the chair, Morgan spotted Pickering coming out of the Hard Rock Saloon. It was getting on toward noon. The tall man adjusted his white hat and walked across the street, past Buck and down several stores. Morgan followed him. He went into a small neat store front that was well painted and had a sign over the door that read: "SILVER QUEEN MINE, Town Office."

Pickering went into the office and closed the door. Morgan walked on past without looking in the windows. This was not a good time. He went into the General Store next door and bought a paper, then a box of .45 rounds and looked at the shotguns. Too damn obvious. Maybe Dunc had one.

He walked back to the Davies house. After his knock on the back door he went inside.

Faith had just finished baking a green apple pie. She ran to him, then stopped and walked ahead slower before she hugged him.

"I'm just so terribly glad every time I see you come back," she said, tears almost brimming out of her eyes.

"I'm glad to be back, too," he said. "That means I'm still alive and fighting." He led her by the hand to the kitchen table and sat her down. Then he put the small notebook in front of her.

"Any idea what these words might mean?" He told her where he found the notebook and the bill of sale for the horse. She stared at them and then slowly shook her head.

"Evidently, you knew that you were coming to Silverville. Somebody must have told you there were mines here and that we had some Chinese. Actually, there aren't any Chinese in town now. Used to have quite a few. Don't know what happened to them. Probably moved out to a new railroad job somewhere. They liked the railroad work better than going down in a mine any day."

"Missing three weeks?" he asked.

"No idea. Maybe someone you're trying to find has been missing in the mines here in Silverville for three weeks. About all I can say."

She jumped up. "You want a piece of warm apple pie with a wedge of cheese and some soon to be whipped cream?"

"Don't ever ask a starving man if he's hungry, woman!"

She grinned and hurried to the stove. The apple pie sat there all cinnamon and sugar coated on the crust and oozing apple goodness through three slits in the top.

They each had a piece of pie after she whipped the cream. Then they sat back and smiled.

"That was your dinner," Faith said. "Not good nutrition, but we'll make up for it at supper. Can I have half of the new paper?"

They both read it then, but it proved to have no story that would help Morgan in his quest. She took his shirt off and checked his back and chest wound.

When she looked at his back, she frowned. "Put your shirt back on," Faith said. "We're going to see Doc Johnson."

"It's not healing?"

"Looks worse now than when it first happened. You need some of his professional treatment."

"No."

"Why not, Morgan?"

"What if Pickering has someone watching the doctor's office for a man coming in shot in the back? He could be there before the doctor got my shirt off."

"Could be. Could also be that you die of blood poisoning. It happened a lot during the big war. You've got the start of a red streak up your back. Blood poisoning doesn't take long, so get your shirt on. We'll go in the back door from the alley. Anyone tries to hurt you, I'll shoot his damned head off."

She fussed in a kitchen drawer and came up with a .32 caliber Smith and Wesson rimfire tip-up revolver. "I said I hated guns, not that I don't have one and can't use it. Yes, it's loaded with four rounds but I don't figure we'll need it." She put it in her reticule.

"Is this really necessary, Faith?"

"Yes. The gun is a safeguard, and as your nurse I'm scared to death the way your back looks. I've never lost a patient, and I don't want you to be my first."

She caught his hand and they went out the back door.

"I'll go ahead. You follow me. Don't get lost, and don't decide to lose me, or you get no more apple pie or fresh baked bread. Deal?"

"Deal."

They got to the doctor's office with no trouble. No one noticed either of them. Morgan waited outside the back door after Faith went in, but he could see no movement up or down the block long alley. After five minutes, he went inside and locked the door behind him.

Faith almost tackled him. "Where have you

been?"

She led him into a small room and a moment later the doctor came in. He was a short man with wild gray hair and a full beard that he kept trimmed close. His forehead bulged slightly accented by a receding hairline. He wore spectacles, the half kind you can look over the top of. Now his sharp blue eyes stared over the top at Faith.

"I see. So this is the father of yours with the cut on his arm. More like a shot in the back. Let's see, let's see."

Buck took off his shirt and the middleaged doctor whistled.

"Be damned. Only saw something like this once before. It was an underpowered .44 with almost no bang left."

He looked from back to front following the path of the slug.

"Should make one Tim Pickering damned mad, fate turning this kind of a trick on him," the doctor said.

"You know about Pickering?" Faith asked.

"Story has been all over town for two days. He told me it was my duty to report any gunshot wounds to the sheriff. Made it plain that if I didn't, he'd have me arrested."

The doctor worked as he talked. He completed taking the dressing off, examined the back wound again.

"You're right, Nurse Davies, it could be the start of blood poisoning, but it isn't, not yet. This is going to hurt, young man."

Almost as he said it, Dr. Johnson swabbed Morgan's back wound with alcohol. Morgan let out a grunt and bit his lips together.

"Everybody is talking about this new problem

called germs," Dr. Johnson said. "Seems these germs we can't see get into a cut or wound and cause all sorts of problems. The alcohol is one way to kill them off. Sorry I had to surprise you. No way to make it hurt less unless I get you drunk first, and we don't have time for that."

As he spoke he swabbed Morgan's chest wound which was not as large and Morgan merely winced.

"Got some good juice here for you to use on him. Twice a day, and make him drink lots of fluids. Probably won't have to come back. Now, young man, what's the matter with your leg?" Doctor Johnson aimed the last question at Buck.

"Mosquito bite."

"Let's look at it."

He pushed up Morgan's pants leg and saw the bandage. When he had it off he shook his head.

"Mosquitoes are growing. This one must be a .45 caliber size. This one looks cleaner." He put some salve on both the wounds and bandaged it again.

"You've got a good nurse there, young man," the doctor said. "I want you to take care of her. Don't let Pickering know where you are. Can you use that Colt on your hip?"

"I shoot some."

"Good. Last man I heard say that was Bat Masterson. I won't be reporting any gunshot wounds, but you stay out of sight. Pickering is mad as hell from what I hear. His job is on the line. Either you're dead or he's hunting work."

"We'll go out the back," Faith said. "Thanks, Dr. Johnson."

Morgan pushed his hand into his pocket and came out with a wad of bills. He dug out a five and handed it to the medical man. The doctor looked surprised.

"Real money? I'm not used to this luxury. Usually I barter my services for eggs, bacon and milk. I'll get change."

"No change, we're even," Morgan said. "Thanks, Dr. Johnson."

They went out singly, Morgan first this time, walking normally, then fading behind a bushy shrub and watching the alley both ways. He could see no hint of danger.

He headed for Faith's house and waited for her at the back door.

"Now," Morgan said. "Tonight we see what kind of action we can stir up in this town. I'm ready to take on Tim Pickering."

# Chapter Six

Tim Pickering stood in front of the heavy oak desk trembling. He was a tall man, about thirty years old, and without a lot of weight or substance. His pants hung on his hips from wide suspenders. He wore a jacket to help fill out his shoulders. He was six-feet two-inches tall but weighed only 165 pounds.

Pickering's face was pale now, his hawk nose looking less severe than usual. Dark eyes wary, his clean shaven jaw quivered slightly. His bony hands turned his white high crowned Stetson around and around but he wasn't aware he was doing it.

"Pickering! Stop turning that damn hat. Drop it on the floor." The one who thundered the order was a huge man, perhaps five-eight and weighing almost 400 pounds. Rolls of fat nearly hid his small brown eyes. His cheeks puffed as he breathed with difficulty. He slumped rather than sat on a huge benchlike chair that had four pillows on it and a large, reinforced back rest also layered with pillows. He was totally bald, his head perfectly smooth and round with no humps or lumps. It was

pristine white since no one could ever remember
Sylvester Bibb being in the sun, or indeed, leaving
his combination office and living quarters.

A huge black man stood impassively behind and
to the right of Bibb. The man helped Bibb move
from place to place, was his servant and companion,
and it was rumored he had once broken a man's
back simply by picking him up and slamming his
back across his knees. Not a flicker of emotion
showed on the ebony face. He was six-four, heavily
muscled and weighed about 240 pounds. There was
no fat anywhere on his body.

Pickering's white hat dropped to the floor on
command. He looked up at his employer.

"Still no word?" the fat man boomed. "Your spies
haven't learned anything yet? It's been more than
forty hours since you failed miserably to do the job
assigned to you."

"I been looking. I've got six people out scouring
the whole town. We took the livery apart, warn't
no body or no wounded man there nowhere."

"You going to smash down every house in town
until you find him?"

"Uh . . . no sir. I guess, maybe not."

"On the other hand, that way you would find the
bastard, wouldn't you?"

"Yes sir, Mr. Bibb."

"You're supposed to be my outside man,
Pickering. I've been putting my trust in you. I'm not
getting my money's worth."

"I did just as you said. We busted him up some,
then he ran out of rounds and I shot him right in
the middle of the back. No way he can't be dead."

"Corpus delecti, Mr. Pickering. Where the hell is
the body? I won't believe Lee Morgan is dead until
I can touch his corpse. Are you significantly clear

on that point?"

Pickering quelled some of his shivering and nodded. "Yes, sir. Yes sir, Mr. Bibb!"

"Pickering, I'm afraid you need a gentle reminder that we are dealing with a tremendously important matter. I've known this man before. The whole future of our endeavor here could be hanging in the balance. You must find him and if he isn't dead, *kill him at once*!"

Bibb caught a bit of drool from his lips as he roared the last of the demand. He turned toward the black man. "Mr. White, one for Mr. Pickering."

The tall, heavy, black man surged toward Pickering with seemingly no effort, swung one massive arm that looked like a big man's thigh. His balled fist hit Pickering in the shoulder and slammed him to the side four-feet before he tumbled to the floor and jolted against the near wall.

"A gentle reminder, Mr. Pickering," Bibb crooned. "Those who fail me simply never have the chance to fail again. If I don't hear that Morgan is dead within the next 18 hours, you'll have to tell Mr. White here why. As you know, he can't speak, except with his hands and feet. I'm sure you know what the outcome of Mr. White's questioning always is."

Pickering got to his knees, then slowly to his feet.

"Yes, Mr. Bibb, I know. I'll . . . I'll go right now and find him, I promise!"

"Do that. I want to know the moment you find him, day or night. But don't wake me up to tell me bad news."

Pickering shook his head and hurried to the door. It opened into an outer office where two heavy faced men sat. Each had a loaded revolver in his holster and a sawed off twin-barreled shotgun primed with double-ought buck on a small shelf near the desk. The shotguns could not be seen over the counter that stretched across the room. It was there more for protection than any other reason.

The men both looked at Pickering, then they relaxed and nodded to him as he went through a locked door in the center of the counter. It could only be unlocked from the inside. Pickering closed it and one of the big men went to lock it.

Pickering took one look behind him at the closed door that shielded him from Mr. Bibb, then he hurried outside.

Behind the closed door, Sylvester Bibb sighed and shook his head. "It is impossible to hire responsible men anymore. Twenty years ago a man could command absolute loyalty from all of his employees, such as I receive from you, Mr. White."

There was no acknowledgement, no flicker in the black eyes. The figure seemed, just then, more like an ebony statue than a man.

Bibb chuckled. "Good, it's after three o'clock, time for my mid afternoon snack. The kitchen, Mr. White."

The black man moved to the back of the chair and pulled it down a foot. Sylvester Bibb lay back with it which freed the front wheels. Then Mr. White rolled it like a wheelbarrow on the large back wheels through a wide pair of double doors and down a five-foot wide hallway to a large kitchen on the right. It had been built with everything at a low level so Bibb could work from his chair.

The big black man seemed to know exactly where the fat man wanted to move. He went from one cupboard to another, then to a chopping block, to the stove which was glowing hot and had a variety of frying pans and pots hanging within reach of the man in the wheeling chair.

In twenty minutes the snack was ready. It included a sear-fried two-pound steak raw in the center, a heap of country fried, previous boiled potatoes, three kinds of vegetables, a half loaf of bread and a jar of jam, plus a quart sized cup of milk.

As Bibb ate, Mr. White stood behind his chair awaiting directions. Most of the orders were given with hand signals that the two had worked out producing a maximum of efficiency.

The mass of food was devoured quickly, then the large man motioned and the black man wheeled the chair into a bedroom. There was no bed. Bibb gave another signal and the chair was lowered to the floor on the front wheels. The whole back of the device unlatched and lowered. It soon rested on swing down legs that touched the floor. The chair was now a nearly flat bed.

Mr. White lowered the blinds in the room, left and closed the door. A moment later another door on the other side of the room opened and two small Chinese girls, thirteen years old, ran up to the big bed. Both girls were naked. They laughed and giggled and crawled on his bed-chair and on him and the after-snack snack began.

The girls chattered in Chinese and it was soon apparent neither could speak English.

The huge man chewed on any breast he could grab and hold. The girls tickled him, held his nose, rubbed his bald head. After five minutes of grabbing and poking and playing with the girls, he clapped his hands once and they turned and ran out the same door they had entered through.

A few moments later, the tall black man came in

and handed Bibb a piece of paper. He read it and swore.

"Not now. Tell him I'm resting, that I can't be disturbed."

The black man ignored the protest, lifted the head of the bed so it moved back into a broad chair. Then he tipped it as before and rolled the bed/chair back to the office area.

When Bibb was situated behind his desk and had some papers spread out in front of him, he nodded at Mr. White. The black man went to the door and opened it.

A man came in wearing a brown suit and holding a brown hat. Under his arm he carried a leather case. He was average height but his body was misshapen as if the pattern was cut slightly askew. His right shoulder tilted down four inches and his left slanted upward four inches. His slightly larger than normal head was tilted perpetually toward the high shoulder.

When he spoke it was with a clipped, superior sounding British accent. "Mr. Bibb, good to see you looking so well today. I'm here with the weekly report. Things are going quite well, actually. Our production rate is up well over what it was last week, and the richness of the ore is actually improving. A wider vein, I believe the tunnel foreman indicated."

He spread out four sheets of figures on the wide desk and pointed to the first one.

"Do you have time for a brandy, Mr. Hyde?" Bibb asked. "I find a brandy particularly refreshing at this time of the day."

"Oh, goodness, no brandy for me. But you go right ahead, sir. I know nothing of spirits. Only mining. But I do know mines. I've been called one of the best mining engineers and general managers that you'll find in the colonies, don't you know."

He waited as Mr. White brought a bottle and poured a brandy glass with a half-inch of the drink. Bibb sniffed the aroma, then swirled the brandy again and took a swallow.

"Ahhhhhhh, yes. Delightful. Now, you've told me what I want to know, production is up. Any kind of trouble, disturbances?"

"None to mention. We did lose one of the workers, but it should be an object lesson to the others. This one had highgrading down to a science. He placed his treasure just beyond the fence each night. Had bribed a guard. Both have been severely disciplined."

"Do you need any more workers?" Bibb asked.

"No, not at the moment. We have two tunnels working and that's the only veins we have to follow now. If one of them branches, we could use another twenty-five. But not yet."

"I still have the contacts in Sacramento."

"Good, good, Mr. Bibb. We shall have some need from simple attrition before long, for say, four a week."

"Anything else?"

"No, sir. I think that tells the story. I'll be back next week about this time." The Englishman stared down at Bibb with a smug, almost superior expression.

"I don't have to remind you, Mr. Bibb, that we are full partners in this endeavor. You'll see my share of the weekly profits plainly spelled out in the report."

"Yes, yes, Mr. Hyde, it always is. But you remember it was my genius that set this up. All you did was the leg work."

"But that is work that you are not able or willing to do yourself, Mr. Bibb. Together we make a good operating team."

"Out, Hyde! Out of my sight, you misshapen, ugly devil of a man!"

Mr. Hyde smiled. "Coming from a mountain of lard, a tub of fat, a monster of the supper table and eight meals a day, I consider that to be a compliment. Good day, sir."

When Mr. Hyde closed the door, the fat man roared with laughter. He had been fat all his life but not this big. That was because he never could afford to eat this much before. He loved being huge. If he could eat enough he might weigh 600 pounds! That was a goal to strive for.

His cook would be here at four and they would go over the menu for the two evening meals, one at six and another at nine. He was looking forward to some really fine gourmet suppers tonight.

Bibb flicked his hand and the ebony tower was beside him. Bibb relaxed as Mr. White rolled him into his parlor where he could look out across an empty lot at the surging mountains to the north. He never tired of watching the mountains and the changing seasons. Now at the height of summer, the mountain held their greenest splendor. The recent rain seemed to brighten everything.

Outside the neatly painted front door of the town office of the Silver Queen Mine, Mr. Hyde turned toward the hotel. He smiled as he anticipated the rest of the afternoon and evening.

The clerk at the hotel put the two dollar bills in his pocket and smiled.

"Yes, sir, Mr. Hyde. Right away. Your usual, but somebody different, I understand. Should take only about 15 minutes. You're in room 22 on the second floor."

The misshapen middleaged man walked to the driveway and up to room 22. Every week he got this same room if it was available. Inside he sat on the bed, then opened the window to let some fresh air into the room.

It wasn't a hot day, not often did it get hot up here. The altitude and the breeze kept things cooled off even in summertime. He took off his hat and put it on the dresser, then his necktie and his jacket and vest, hanging each carefully on a wire coat hanger.

Hyde sat beside the window looking down on Main Street. Mining towns were all alike, but this one was slightly better simply because it had been here longer.

The knock on the door came before he thought it would. When he opened the door he saw two women outside. One was tall and slender, had henna red hair and freckles. The other one was younger, maybe 25, with large breasts and soft blonde hair around her shoulders.

"Ladies, I do believe that you've come to the right place. Won't you please step inside."

"Ya really wanted two of us?" the older, taller one asked, her voice like sliding gravel.

"Oh, absolutely. I haven't seen either of you before. Is that correct?"

They nodded.

"We don't do nothing outlandish or that will hurt us," the younger one said.

"Ladies, I'm sure you don't. My name is Horace. Yes, one of my shoulders is tipped up and the other one down. It doesn't affect my mind at all. I'm a mining engineer and you are each earning ten dollars for yourselves and ten dollars for the saloon. Does that sound interesting?"

"Sure," the older one said with some enthusiasm. "Christ, I'll do anything for ten bucks."

"Good, the blind is down, let's start with names."

"I'm Cathy Lee," the older one said.

"Ruth," the other one.

"Fine, now Ruth, I want you to lie down on the bed." He waited for her to do it. "Take off your shoes. Now Cathy Lee, sit on the side of the bed. It takes me awhile to get excited, ladies. To help me, I want the two of you to make love. Undress each other and then have sex with each other."

Ruth sat up. "Ain't that unnatural?"

"Not at all, Ruth, what can it hurt? You do want that ten dollars, don't you? All I'll do right now is watch."

"Hell, why not? You done it before, Ruth. Told me once. I think it might be fun for a change," Cathy Lee said. She bent forward and kissed Ruth on the lips and reached for her big breasts. Slowly, Ruth let Cathy Lee push her backwards to the bed and quickly the older woman had pulled open Ruth's blouse and was fondling her full breasts with nipples as round as a thumb.

Horace moved his chair closer to the bed and sat there watching. After awhile his hands went down to his crotch and he rubbed slowly. It would take awhile. It always did for him. But he had plenty of time, all night.

He watched at Cathy Lee slowly seduced Ruth. Their dresses came off and the two women looked at each other for a moment. Then Ruth closed her eyes, caught Cathy Lee's head and brought her mouth down to her big breasts. Cathy Lee sucked one in her mouth and made small noises in her throat.

Already Ruth was grinning, and reached for

Cathy Lee's smaller breasts, tweaking the nipples, petting them, watching as they grew in size.

As he watched them, Horace began to take off his shirt. He worked at it slowly. Before he had it off, Ruth had pulled Cathy Lee off her breast and pushed her head down to her crotch. Cathy Lee moaned with delight as Ruth spread her legs, showing a blonde fur patch and pink nether lips.

Cathy Lee gave a small cry and pressed her mouth over the pinkness. Ruth thrilled in pleasure and fell backwards on the bed.

At last, Horace felt a lump rising in his crotch. He grinned. Oh, yes, this was going to be a fine night. He thought of the whip and the ropes and chains he had in his suitcase and he smiled a devilish mask. This was going to be a wonderful night!

# Chapter Seven

Tim Pickering was not a brave man. He hated being called on the carpet that way by Mr. Bibb. But the man was right, he did owe his employer an honest day's work. He rubbed his shoulder where the black giant had hit him. Pickering had been smart enough to know it was coming and he jolted sideways just as the blow came.

He had done it before. The effect was a hard push rather than the battering blow it looked like. Mr. White didn't care if they fooled Bibb. Pickering sometimes felt he saw a glint of satisfaction when they put something over on the fat man.

Now Pickering set his jaw and marched down the street to the Hard Rock Saloon. Few in town knew it, but Mr. Bibb owned the saloon and seven or eight other business firms in the community.

He pushed past the bar and into the back room where two men sat at a table playing cards and a woman lounged on a couch with heavy cushions.

"Trouble," Pickering said. "We find Morgan in eighteen hours or we're all out of work." He grabbed the woman by one arm and pulled her to her feet. "That means you, too, Big Tits. We all get on the street and find the bastard!"

The woman had been combing her hair. She was in her twenties, plump, and wore a skirt and a blouse that barely covered her surging breasts.

"What can I do?" she mewed.

"Go to all the whore houses in town and show them that picture on the wanted poster and see if any of the girls have seen him. He's bound to need a woman sooner or later."

He stared at the other two. One was Shorty, he was nearly six-feet tall and slender as a hoe handle. Twin revolvers hung on slender hips. His face was thin and strained as if he didn't eat enough. He didn't, because he drank his meals out of a whiskey bottle. His eyes were just a bit bleary.

"Damn! Told you I should have checked him the other night after you shot him," Shorty said.

Pickering put all of his weight into his blow as he powered a fist into Shorty's shoulder. The man didn't see it coming and it slammed him across a chair and into the table which fell over as Shorty crashed to the floor.

"You remind me once more, and you're the one we'll be digging a grave for. Christ, how many times you going to tell me that? Shorty, work the saloons again, no more than ten minutes in any of them, and keep going to one after another until they close tonight. And no booze until we nail the bastard. I find you with a drink in your hand and you're a dead man! Get out of here."

Shorty got up, brushed off his clothes and walked out the door with a scowl.

"You're next, Tits. Get moving or the free ride is over and you're back to working with your ass. Get out there now."

The woman scowled, put on a light sweater to cover herself a little better and left.

Pickering stared at the other man who still toyed with the deck of playing cards. He was a wide-shouldered square-cut man who looked like a brawler. He was.

"So why are you still here, Nate?"

"Cause I know where Bilbray will be at four o'clock today. He's got to go see the banker."

Pickering grinned for the first time in a half hour. "Yeah, got the bastard. You and Shorty know where to be, the alley. Yeah! Now, this other matter. Bilbray won't matter much if we don't find Morgan. Where else is there to look?"

"Hotels, restaurants, he know anybody in town?" Nate asked.

"Not that we know of. He's a loner. Come to do a job and now we lost the bastard."

"I'll check the streets, the stage, the stores, but most of all, the eating places," Nate said. "He's got to eat somewhere."

"That's what worries me. He is eating somewhere. You suppose some citizen found him and took him in and is taking care of him? I'll talk with Doc Johnson again. I can tell if that old sawbones is lying. Let's get it done. We've got to find that bastard Morgan."

At the doctor's office, Pickering pushed aside the doctor's wife and barged into a room where the medic was bandaging a man's arm.

"Pickering, might have guessed," Doctor Johnson said. "What do you want?"

"You know. You treated any gunshot wounds yesterday or today?"

"Why would I tell you?"

"Because if you don't, I just might mess up your face with my fists. Can you set your own broken nose?"

"Easily. Can you repair your own heart after it takes a .45 slug through it?"

Pickering looked down and saw the six-gun in the doctor's hand.

"Move out the door and right on out of my office or I'll put a round through your leg and I won't treat it. Take your choice, move or get shot. I'm through letting you push me around."

"You couldn't do it, Doc. Not a chance."

The .45 went off in the small room and it sounded like a cannon. The hot led snarled through Pickering's pants leg narrowly missing flesh.

"Still think I'm bluffing, Pickering? I'm damn good with one of these things. The next one will go through your thigh and I'll be aiming at the bone. You want a broken leg, too?"

Pickering began to back out the door. "All right, just relax. I didn't touch you."

"And I won't touch you, Pickering, but some hot lead damn well will. Out!" The doctor kept the weapon trained on the man until he pushed out the back door and into the alley. Then the furious doctor fired three times beside and behind Pickering as the tall, thin man ran at full speed down the alley.

Two blocks down the street, Nate had folded over the wanted poster of Buckskin Morgan so it showed only the picture. He let the waitresses in the hotel restaurant look at it, but both of them shook their heads. They hadn't seen him.

"Handsome man like that I would have remembered," the younger one of the two said. "He sure ain't been eating here."

Nate tried the three cafes in town with the same results. They would know. Morgan had not been eating at any of them. That meant he'd been staying with a family somewhere in town.

Nate gave up and went into the General Store, but still drew a blank. He checked in at the three other saloons, and ran into Shorty, but he was having no luck either.

The woman, whose real name was Fanny, was still in the first saloon that had girls. She was having a drink with a miner who couldn't keep his hands out of her blouse.

"Told you I'm retired, not in the business any-more," Fanny said with a grin.

"Yeah, yeah, you'll never retire. You like getting poked too much."

"Not by you." She finished the beer, rubbed his crotch and went upstairs to talk to the girls. All four came out of their rooms within the next half hour. They looked at the picture on the poster and shook their heads.

"Wasting your time, Fanny," a faded soiled dove called Princess told her. "A gent like him won't be paying for his loving, you can count on that. He's got some little sweetie all bundled in the haymow somewhere. We'll never see him."

"Yeah, my luck. Without him my man is about done in for good. You got room for another girl here?"

"Think you can still stand the grabbing and pawing and stink of these miners?"

"Used to, guess I can again. Where's my crib?"

"Anyone that's not got the door locked, just as it always been. You sure, Fanny?"

Fanny grinned, shrugged. "Yes, I'm sure. I better get to work."

Outside on the street, Tim Pickering walked the short three blocks of the town's shopping area, watching faces. He had the features of Buckskin Morgan burned into his brain. He almost drew on one man, but when he turned fully around the face wasn't right.

Twice he almost got into fights when he lifted hats on men who had them pulled down on their faces. Neither man was Morgan.

As he walked, he watched the time. He needed to end up in the middle of the street outside the dentist's office right at four o'clock.

Bilbray wouldn't be able to back down. Not with the big mouth he'd had around town lately. It was a matter of honor, of living up to what you claimed you were going to do. For a week now, Bilbray had been trying to get the people stirred up to run Tim Pickering out of town.

He even tried to get a court order, but the judge wouldn't be through here for two more months. The deputy sheriff laughed at him, then quickly told Pickering about the legal try. Now was when the braggart had to answer directly for his big mouth, had to put his six-gun in back of his accusations.

Four o'clock in front of the dentist's office.

Pickering moved down the street and went into the Watchmaker and Jewerly Shop. The bell on the door tinkled and a face came up from the workbench behind a small counter.

"Dunc, is my watch ready yet?" Pickering asked.

Dunc Davies looked up, startled at first to find the man they had been so concerned about right there in the shop. He let the eyepiece fall out of his right eye and blinked as he always did.

"Yes, let's see, Pickering, right? That was a nicely made silver pocket watch for cleaning and setting.

Looks like it's all ready. That'll be a dollar."

"A dollar? Damn, last time cost only fifty cents."

"Let that be a lesson. Keep it away from moisture. Looked like it could have been dunked in water even. Had to scrape off some rust and work over some of the mechanism. But she'll run like a railroad now."

"Yeah, all right." Pickering gave him a dollar and looked at the time. "This set right?"

"Down to the tenth of a second. Right now it's three, forty-two and about eighteen seconds."

Pickering looked at the timepiece, put the leather thong around his belt loop and let the watch sink into his pocket.

"Yeah, close enough." He turned and walked out of the shop without a goodbye.

Dunc watched him go. He seemed to be in a hurry now. One of these days Buck was going to catch him without his friends and settle their small shoot-in-the back problem.

Outside, Pickering paced down the boardwalk faster now. He didn't see the step up at the General Store walk and tripped, nearly sprawling on the boards. Someday all of the levels of these damn walks had to be the same, he told himself.

He made it to the dentist's office five minutes before four o'clock. He peered inside but saw no one in the small waiting room just inside the door. The dentist was new in town, and Pickering had no idea what his name was. The sign simply said "General Dentistry." It had been there through the last three dentists Pickering could remember.

Pickering leaned against the front of the blacksmith shop next door and waited. He unsnapped the leather strap that held his six-gun in the holster and trailed the leather down behind his leg. Then he eased the weapon in and out of the holster twice to be sure it moved easily with no hangups.

Two minutes later he saw the slightly bow legged man with the little pot belly come rolling down the boardwalk. He had on a pair of cotton trousers and a checkered shirt. On his right hip hung a holster filled with iron. Pickering grinned.

When Bilbray was six feet away, Pickering moved onto the boardwalk directly in front of him.

"Mr. Bilbray, I'd say we have an argument to settle. Don't you think this would be a good day to take care of it?"

"No. I mean yes, we have an argument, but I won't draw against you."

"In that case it'll be easy for me, won't it? I'm going to shoot you down, Bilbray. You might as well have the satisfaction of trying to outdraw and outshoot me."

"You're too fast."

"Should have thought of that when you kept spreading those lies about me. Out into the street, Bilbray. No reason to shoot up any store windows."

Bilbray hesitated. His lower lip trembled. Sweat beaded just under his old felt hat. His right hand twitched as he looked down at the gunman's low tied holster.

"It's no better than murder, Pickering." His voice raised to a shout. "This man Pickering is trying to kill me!" he shouted.

One or two people turned, but most of the towns folks within hearing went on their way.

"You could be next!" Bilbray screamed. "You, Halsteen the butcher, he could get mad at you next and call you out." The man called Halsteen never turned around.

"Where's the Deputy Sheriff?" Bilbray screeched.

"I demand to have the Deputy here."

"He's busy right now," Pickering said. "You moving into the street, or you want to die right there on the boardwalk?"

Bilbray kept looking around. No one came to his aid. At last he groaned and stepped into the street.

'It's murder, plain and simple. Murder!"

The dentist's office was right beside where the alley cut back through from Main Street. The narrow slot between buildings was murky with afternoon shadows.

The two men stood in the street now, twenty feet apart.

"I'll make it easy for you, Bilbray," Pickering said. "I'm gonna count to three, then draw. You go ahead and draw just anytime you want to, Mr. Bilbray. One." He waited a moment. "Two . . . Three."

Pickering was moderately fast.

Morgan had come out of a saloon across the street and stared at the scene. He'd seen it many times before. This was familiar. He saw Pickering's right hand dart down for his weapon, grab it and pull it free and lift it.

The shot that rang out seemed a little fast and almost in the same moment he heard what he swore were two other shots. The second man in the street facing Pickering never got his weapon out of the holster. He jolted to the side, then slammed to the rear where he sprawled on the dust filled street and never moved again.

A curious crowd gathered when the gunplay was over. Somebody went up to the man on the ground and looked at the body, then rolled him over.

"Right through the heart!" the man said. "Damn, that was good shooting."

A man with a star on his chest came through the crowd. He looked around.

"What happened here?" he asked.

"A shootout, Deputy," the man who had checked the body said. "Looked like self defense. Both of them drew at the same time."

The deputy looked at Pickering who had walked forward. "That right?" he asked Pickering.

"Yeah, Deputy. He called me out and we talked and he started to draw and damned if I didn't beat him."

"Come down to the office. You'll have to sign a statement." The Deputy was a stout man with a fat little belly. He pointed to two men. "You and you, get that body down to the undertakers."

Morgan scratched his jaw. Why would a body jolt to the side when it was shot from the front? Answer, it wouldn't. He wandered down a dozen feet to the alley and stepped into the shadows. He sniffed and at once knew why the body had been rocked to the left.

He smelled the unmistakable odor of gunpowder smoke. Somebody had shot from the alley just before Pickering had fired. The shots came close enough together to make it hard to tell them from one round.

Morgan eased along behind the men who carried the dead man. He saw where they were going and waited ten minutes after they came out of the office before he went in.

The undertaker was a small round man with a red face, fringes of red hair, spectacles and a perpetual smile.

He looked up as Morgan slipped through the office door into the room where the corpse laid on a table.

"Sorry, nobody allowed back here," the man said still smiling.

"Sorry yourself, but I just have a quick question for you. How many slugs you find in that body?"

"Hell, one, right in the heart. Why?"

"Check his left side," Buck said.

"Check . . . who are you, anyway? Why should I check?"

"Take a look, you have to take his clothes off anyway. Take a look."

"Hell, if only to get rid of you." The undertaker unbuttoned the man's shirt and pulled it out of his pants and lifted up a light undershirt.

"Be damned!" the body carver said. "Look at that! Two more bullet holes in his side." The undertaker looked up quickly. "You some kind of lawman or something?"

"Not so you could notice. Just thought it strange when I hear three shots at a shootout and the winner fires only one and the loser none at all. You don't need to mention this to anyone. Be better for your health if you don't."

Lee pulled his six-gun and laid it next to the red face of the little man pressing the muzzle ever so lightly against his head.

"You mention to anybody that I was in here asking about this, you'll be your own next customer. Understand?"

The small man with the fringes of red hair nodded. When Morgan eased out the door into the office, the Silverville undertaker was still nodding his sweating head.

# Chapter Eight

Morgan left the undertaker's establishment and meandered around on the street where the shooting had taken place, but did not see Pickering. The two of them had to have a serious "nigh unto death talk" and the sooner the better. But maybe not today.

Morgan turned back toward the Davies house. He still wished that he could remember. Damnit! He was walking around like a blind man. Maybe Dunc had some information for him. He felt like he was just half a man not knowing his background, where he had been or what he had done. All just one big damn blank page.

An hour later they sat around the supper table in the Davies' house. Here he felt at home, safe, secure. Faith had put on a pretty blouse and combed out her long brown hair until it shone in a tawny wave around her shoulders. Whenever she glanced up at him now she had an expression he recognized at once. He knew the look and wasn't sure that he objected. One afternoon making love with him and she wanted him to stay and be with her for the rest of her life. He had seen the expression on women's faces before and before he had been terrified by it. Now it didn't seem to be so bad.

Dunc had started talking as soon as he got in the door that evening.

"The other mine in this area is the Big Strike Number One. You know that. The man who runs it is Janish Lang, about my age. Far as I know, he's honest, realiable, a good man. His mine is closer to town, about a quarter-a-mile, and the men walk out or ride every day to go to work. Seems he runs a good operation, is making money and we just never hear much bad about him. He lives right here in town."

"He comes to church, is married, has a family and seems like a nice man," Faith said.

"You've probably been thinking the same thing I have," Dunc said. "Somebody in town must have hired you to come here. If Bibb and his gunmen tried to stop you, it must mean that it was Lang who hired you."

"So I should go see this Mr. Lang and come right out and ask him if he hired a fast gun?" Morgan asked.

Dunc nodded. "Don't rightly see any other way to figure out exactly why you're here." Dunc remembered the wanted poster and squirmed. He probably should tell Buck he was wanted, but he didn't think this was the right time. Anyway, those posters could be put out by anybody.

Morgan worked on the thick steak, mashed potatoes and gravy and three kinds of vegetables. "I know I'm getting fat eating this well, Faith. Tomorrow, let's have burned biscuits, hard fried eggs and maybe some greasy strips of bacon. I'd feel more at home."

She smiled at him and he could see a cottage with curtains in the windows and three kids waving at him from the door. He shook his head to get rid of the image.

Lang lives right here in town," Dunc said. "Fact is, he's down the street just a couple of blocks. Nice house but not a palace."

"Does he have guards and fences and dogs protecting him?" Morgan asked.

"Not at all." Dunc said. "No guards at all, I know of. Just a regular man like the rest of us."

Morgan sipped at his second cup of coffee.

"All right, it's decided. Right after supper, I'll go over there and see this Mr. Janish Lang. Might be able to clear up a lot of things that way."

He waited until almost seven-thirty, then headed for the address Dunc gave him. It was a modest house for a mine owner, wooden construction, three stories and painted white. No fence, no door bell. He knocked sharply three times and waited. Lights were just starting to come on around town.

A moment later someone came to the door. When it opened a man looked out. He was shorter than Morgan, had thinning hair and a broad smile.

"Yes sir, can I help you?" Lang asked.

"Mr. Janish Lang?"

"Yes, that's right."

"Could I talk to you for a minute?"

A frown flickered across the man's face, then he nodded and stepped back and Buck moved inside the house and the door closed.

"Mr. Lang, I don't know quite how to start. Did you send out of the area to hire a man to come and work for you, a man who had some experience with guns?"

Lang looked up quickly. "I sure as hell did. But I hear that Pickering and his gang of thugs shot down the man. Too damn bad, I needed him."

"Mr. Lang, what was the man's name you hired?"

Lang looked at him closely. "Not sure that should be any of your business. Why don't you tell me who you are and why you're interested in this man I tried to hire."

"Mr. Lang, that's part of my problem. I'd like to tell you who I am, but I rightly don't know. My new friends here in town tell me that I was in a fight with six men and then Tim Pickering shot me. But somewhere along the action, I lost my memory."

"Pickering shot you? You could be the man I hired. Does Idaho mean anything to you? A place called Grove, Idaho?"

Lee furrowed his brow, then shook his head. "Sorry, doesn't seem familiar at all."

"Damn! Well, come into my den, I'll show you a copy of the letter I wrote and see if that stirs any memories. If Pickering and his goons beat you up and shot you, I'd say it's more than likely that you're the man I sent for."

Down the hall way they came to a den with heavy furniture, a desk, a globe on a stand, and one wall covered with bookcases that were well-filled. Lang lit a lamp on the desk and looked through a drawer a moment.

Then he brought out a piece of paper. "Not too good with my handwriting. I'll read it to you. It's addressed to Lee Buckskin Morgan, Grove, Idaho." He looked up sharply. "That name mean anything to you, young man?"

Buck shook his head. "Friends here in town call me Buck, but that's just a coincidence."

Lang gave him a long look. "Maybe. Date on this

copy of the letter is two months ago. I asked Buckskin Morgan to come here to Silverville to help me with a problem I have. Another mine operator in the area has a fast gun who is hurting me and my miners. Also, this other miner is turning out twice the ore that I am and I want to know how he's doing it." He looked up from the paper. "That's about all there was. I also offered you a thousand dollars for a month's work if you can help me with these two problems."

"I don't hire out for straight killing jobs," Buckskin said. "You can find plenty who will do that." He stopped and looked up at Lang. "Now where did those words come from? Must be the real me talking there. I didn't think that through, it just blurted out."

"Good, good," Lang said. "I think part of your memory is coming back. Your name is Lee Buckskin Morgan. You come from Idaho where you have a ranch."

"Yeah, the Spade Bit, where me and my dad raise horses, only my dad is gone now, killed in a shoot-out."

Lang watched him. "Had you known that before, about the Spade Bit?"

Morgan began to grin. "Not a particle of it. Another sentence just busted out of my lips. I think my old brain is trying to help me get my memory back."

Lang pulled a bottle from his desk. "Could you use a spot of sipping whiskey?"

"Rightly so, Mr. Lang. I'm feeling better than I have since I woke up two days ago after Pickering shot me in the back."

Lang looked up suddenly. "Shot you in the back two days ago and you're up and moving?"

"You won't believe this either. I better show you."

Five minutes later Morgan had stripped off his shirt and showed Lang the entry point and how the bullet traveled around his rib and came out.

"Be damned! I never would have believed it if I hadn't seen it."

"Pickering can't believe it either. So you see, I've got a personal score to settle with him. I'm not too fond of back shooters, especially when it's me who gets shot and I'm half unconscious laying in the mud and rain on my belly."

Lang tossed down the rest of his glass of whiskey and paced the den. "Buck, I'm sure you're my man. Can you use that iron you have tied down?"

"I shoot some."

Lang chuckled. "Only good men with a gun say that. So, Pickering is covered. How can we find out what's going on up at the Silver Queen mine Bibb owns? They have fences and rifle toting guards around the place day and night."

"Talk to the men who work there."

"That's part of the problem. The workers up there live up there. It's near ten miles into the hills from here. Only other mine in this stretch that isn't worked out. Nobody seems to know where he gets his diggers, or anything about them."

"What about the law in this area?" Morgan asked. "How does Pickering get away with his gun talk?"

"Almost no law here. Don't know if you've met our deputy sheriff. He's about as close to no law as you can get. I'm sure that he's on Bibb's payroll at three or four times what the county pays him. We're in El Dorado County, but the county seat is over twenty miles away. The Sheriff has been to town only once."

Now it was Morgan's turn to walk the room.

"How did you hear about me? What did you hear?"

"If you're the same man, and I'm about convinced that you are, I heard about you in Sacramento. The word was that if there was an especially tough job to be done, you were the best man in the West to do it. I heard you spent some of your time at the Mile High Hotel in Denver," Lang said.

"Denver? I can't ever remember being there," Morgan said.

"That's where I mailed your letter. The hotel evidently knew you and forwarded it to you wherever you were."

"That's possible."

"People I talked to said you were good with a six-gun, but that you weren't over the edge. They said you used a little style and conscience in your work," Lang said.

Morgan laughed. "Nice to learn all these things about myself. What if I'm not this guy after all? I could have gunned down this Morgan, taken the letter and come here for the job. How would you know the difference?"

Lang rubbed his hand over his face, then stared at Morgan for a moment. "Possible, yes, but I don't think so. I think I'm a good judge of character, and I don't see anything to make me believe you aren't the man I sent for." He sat down in the big chair behind the desk.

"At any rate, the job is yours, if you want it. The thousand dollar offer still stands. I need to get a little breathing room here. Pickering is either chasing out of town or shooting down two of my workers a week. I can't stand for that."

Morgan turned and held out his hand. "Deal," he said. "I like the way you lay your cards on the table. I'll see what I can find out about the Bibb mine, and

I'll damn well put Pickering out of business. I'm not sure which one first but I'll dig into both the problems for you."

The men shook hands and Lang smiled. "I'm pleased. I think you can do both jobs. How you fixed for cash? You need any advance on your wages?"

"No. I'll do the job first. If Pickering is faster than I think he is, or if he gets me in the back again, you won't be out any money."

They had one more shot of the sipping whiskey, then Morgan asked if he could go out the back door just in case anyone was watching the front. No sense in taking any chances. He slipped into the blackness and waited. Nothing moved. No sound came. He waited for five minutes, then headed down the alley toward the Davies house.

He was starting to remember. The Spade Bit in Idaho. He didn't do straight killing jobs. Yes, a little was coming back, slowly. His brain must have been really scrambled. Pickering was going to pay for this, not just a straight shootout. There had to be something special for Mr. Pickering. Something damn special.

It was still early. Maybe he could find the sonofabitch tonight.

Morgan checked one saloon but saw that Pickering wasn't there. He left and went to the Hard Rock Saloon, bought a beer and sat with his back to the wall working on the mug of suds. He waited fifteen minutes, then he got restless. He didn't know why, but he figured he shouldn't stay there any longer. He went out the back door leaving his beer half finished on the table. He didn't care who noticed.

When he got to the alley he hurried his pace and then he was running. Why? He wasn't sure. It was a damn bad feeling he had in his bones. Something was wrong. Something was wrong at the Davies' house.

He picked up his pace, felt his leg screaming at him with pain but he battered down the knifing sensations and ran faster toward the Davies' house. He just knew that he had to get back there as fast as he could.

# Chapter Nine

If Morgan hadn't surprised them, he and Faith and Dunc would all be dead.

He ran up to the front of the house. It was closest. It was the fastest way to get inside from downtown. That was what saved them all.

Morgan was panting when he stopped just short of the front porch. He bent over to get his breath and to try to slow down the daggers from searing through his right leg and even his arm now.

He already had the six-gun in his hand. With the double action Colt .45, he didn't have to cock it between each round. The trigger pull cocked the hammer and then let it fall. He could fire five times as fast as he could pull the trigger.

Morgan stood straight and eased up the steps to the front door. It was never locked. He turned the knob silently and pushed the door inward a half inch. No chair, no bolt, no chain. He edged the panel inward a full inch and listened through the crack.

He heard a woman sobbing. Faith.

Two voices mumbled low and in the background.

Where were they? Inside somewhere, not watching the front door. So they would be in the kitchen or the bedroom. He eased the door inward again six inches so he could see past it down the short hallway.

Nothing there.

He stepped in. The floorboards creaked. Sweat popped out on his forehead in a nervous reflexive action.

He hoped the voices in back blocked out the floorboards noise. Morgan lifted the six-gun and stepped forward. Nobody in the small living room. Beyond that the kitchen. He could see no one. There was a lamp burning in the kitchen.

They had to be in the bedrooms. One of the two. Closest one was Faith's. He remembered it well.

Before he could move a man stepped out of Faith's bedroom and saw him. The stranger swung up a sawed off shotgun and his finger touched the trigger just as Morgan fired. His round ripped through Shorty's chest, plowing a wide hole through his heart and out his back.

A hundredth of a second after Morgan fired, Shorty's dead trigger finger spasmed forward on the trigger, dropping the hammer. The double-ought buck round exploded, most of the .32 caliber size pellets thundered into the wooden floor. Two of them bounced off and one hit Morgan's boot heel nearly knocking his foot out from under him.

For a moment after the shotgun blast the echoes dribbled off to total silence. Morgan stepped around the hall partition into the living room just as a shotgun poked out of Faith's room and blasted a round of double-ought buck down the hallway. It was followed by the sound of someone smashing a window.

"Getting away!" Morgan growled. He charged down the hallway into Faith's room in time to see the last of a man vanishing over the window sill and into the darkness. He charged to the window and fired four more times at the figure running away into the darkness before Morgan's weapon ran dry.

Only then did he look around the room.

On the bed lay Faith, naked and tied spread eagled to the bedframe. Her eyes were red. His boot knife came out and Morgan slashed the torn up sheets that kept her tied to the bed.

"Look for Pa!" Faith shouted as he cut her bounds. "He must be in the kitchen."

They ran to the kitchen and found Dunc sprawled on the kitchen floor on his face. Faith knelt beside him. Morgan had reloaded his Colt as they ran. Now he turned over Dunc Davies. He was still alive. His breath came in gasps. A bloody bullet hole in his chest must have just missed his heart but cut a torturous hole through his lung.

"I'll go get Doc," Faith said. Then she realized she was still naked.

"Get that shooting iron of yours, get a dress on and watch the front door," Morgan ordered. "I'll run and get Doc Johnson. Don't want to move Dunc right yet until the Doc looks at him. It's bad, you know it's bad."

"Hell yes, bad," Dunc said. "Where you two been?"

Morgan caught Faith's hand and held it. He looked at Dunc. "You're still alive. Figured it'd take more than one slug to kill an old watchmaker like you. Faith, you watch him. Don't move, Dunc. Doctor will be right here. Remember who the bastards were. I got one, the tall bean pole."

Then Morgan hurried out the back door. He went

down two alleys and came out half a block from the doctor. He knocked on the door and a light flared.

Two minutes later Doctor Johnson was walking rapidly beside Morgan toward the Davies' house.

"Hit him high in the chest, left side you said. Must have missed his heart."

Morgan gritted his teeth as he walked. His leg must have broken open. It hurt like hell.

They went through the back door, calling to Faith as they did. She had put a pillow under Dunc's head and a blanket over him. She also had on a dress and shoes.

"He said he was cold," Faith said.

Doc Johnson went to his knees and began checking Dunc. He looked up. "Did you notice if the slug came out Dunc's back?"

"Didn't see any sign of blood, but we really didn't look," Morgan said. They eased him to his side and Doctor Johnson's hand explored his back. At last he nodded.

"Yes, a small exit wound lower down. Good, we won't have to dig in there after it."

"Suits me fine, Doc," Dunc said. "How's your garden this year?"

"Dunc, glad you're still with us. Just so you'll stay around a while I don't want you to talk any more for a spell. Have you spit up any blood?"

Dunc shook his head.

"Hurt to breathe?"

Dunc nodded.

"We're going to get you into bed, then I'll see what the hell I can do to help you. Not an awful lot, I'm afraid. Fifty years from now medicine will know exactly what to do. Guess I was just born too early in the century."

It took them ten minutes to get Dunc into his bedroom. At last they let him stand up slowly, then had him walk.

"Can't put any pressure on your chest," Doc told him.

When they had him bedded down and bandaged, they turned down the lamp and went into the kitchen where Faith had coffee going. Doc turned to Faith, his face serious.

"Now, for you, young lady. Did you get hurt?"

"No, just scared half to death."

"That's easy to treat. Did they rape you?"

Faith looked quickly at Morgan, then lifted her brows. "No, Doc. Buck got here in time to stop them. That's part of the scared to death part."

"Same treatment." He walked up to her and put his arms around her and held her tightly. At last he bent and kissed her cheek and stepped back.

"Now, is that better? What I call H & K care. Works every time. H & K stand for hugs and kisses. As for Dunc, we can only hope. He looks good right now. If that round went through high enough up in his lung it won't do a lot of damage. He'll be sore for a week or so, and if there's no infection from those damn little unseen germ things, he should be fine.

"You keep him home for at least a week and let me know if he spits up blood or has any trouble breathing, wheezing, that sort of thing."

Faith nodded and walked the doctor to the door. Morgan brought out a ten dollar bill and gave it to the medic.

"You're downright spoiling me, Buck. While I'm here let me look at your various cuts and bullet holes."

He checked over Morgan in the living room, changed the dressing and worried a minute over the leg wound.

"Don't look the best, but might come out all right. I'll look again in three days."

They let the medic out the front door and Faith ran into Morgan's arms. She began to cry softly and he took her to the couch where they sat down.

"They were waiting for you to come back," she said. "They told us they would kill you and then us too. When you didn't come right away they started touching me and feeling me. Then they tied me on the bed and they cut off my clothes! I've never been so angry or frightened in my life.

"Pa kept yelling at them and fighting with them. Finally he went at them with a knife, and the tall one shot Pa with his pistol almost point blank.

"Then they took me to the bed and tied me down. I don't know who the tall one was but the heavy set one was called Nate. He's almost as tall as you are with big shoulders and arms."

"Good, I have a name and description." He bent and kissed her cheek and then held her tightly for a minute.

"Now, I have to clean up some trash. You stay right here." He went to the body in the hallway and picked up the sawed off double barreled shotgun. He found half a dozen rounds in the dead man's pockets. Then he boosted the body on his shoulder and carried it out the back door and down the alley. He walked with him two blocks over and dumped him alongside the street.

Back at the house, he found some blood spots on his vest and washed them out the best he could.

Faith still lay on the couch. She had curled up with her head on a pillow. "I think I'll sleep right here tonight," she said.

"We'll talk about that later. I'm going hunting.

Not sure when I'll be back. You lock all the doors and windows and don't let anyone in. Keep that five-shot revolver in your hand and use it if you need to."

He hefted the sawed off shotgun, slid the extra shells in his pocket and reloaded the one fired barrel. Morgan slipped on the ankle length duster and hung the shotgun by a rawhide thong around his neck. The duster covered the scatter gun and its ten-inch barrel completely. He put a sixth round in his Colt and then stepped out the back door and headed for saloon row.

In the first three drinking emporiums he found no one who even looked like he could be Nate. In two of the saloons he asked the apron if he had seen his old buddy Nate. The barkeeps simply shook their heads and looked away. Nate was not well liked in the community.

The Hard Rock Saloon had been most productive finding Pickering so he went back there. These two men must be working with Pickering. He bought a beer and sat under his slouch hat for ten minutes in the Hard Rock before he saw Pickering himself slide into the saloon and vanish past the bar and into a back room.

Interesting, Morgan decided. Pickering moved like he owned the place. Another man came in, large, broad shouldered, with arms the size of oak limbs. He had to be the one. He wore a pistol on his hip but it didn't look much used. The man stepped up to the bar and got a beer but didn't pay for it. Figured.

Morgan took the small notebook from his pocket and wrote on it with a stub pencil.

"Nate: You hunting that guy who got shot in the rain couple days ago? I know where he is. Meet me in the alley in back of this place, right now."

Morgan found a man deep in his cups with an empty beer mug. He showed the note to the man and waved a quarter at him.

"You take this note to the barkeep and I'll give you a quarter. You understand?"

The drunk grabbed at the quarter. Morgan had written "Nate" on the outside of the note and folded it over once. The drunk sobered up a little, stared at the note, then at Buck.

"Take the paper to the apron . . . and I get the quarter."

"Right. I'll be watching you. If you don't do it, I'll throw you out into the street."

"Yeah, yeah."

Morgan made him repeat his orders again, then gave him the quarter and the note. Morgan moved toward the back door but stayed in a spot where he could see the bar. The drunk stumbled once, almost dropped the note, but at last got to the bar. He threw the note on the glistening top and yelled at the apron.

The bar man came over and looked at the name on the note, picked it up and glared at the drunk, then shrugged and carried the paper down the bar where the big shouldered man sipped on his beer. He read the note, looked around and the barkeep pointed at the drunk.

Two minutes later Nate must have figured out he wasn't going to learn from the drunk who gave him the note. He snorted, lifted the six-gun from his holster and angled for the back door. Morgan was right behind him. As soon as Nate pushed open the outside door, Morgan drove into him from behind, hitting him in the back with his shoulder, slamming the stocky man through the door and face down in the dirt of the alley.

The six-gun in his hand skidded away into the darkness. Morgan rolled off the man, cringing at the pain in his left arm, and came up with his own weapon trained on the other man.

"We have a nice little talk right here Nate, or you die slow. How does that sound?"

"You're Buckskin Morgan, right?"

"I ask the questions, Nate. Don't get up, stay right there, face down on the dirt, where you belong."

Morgan put his foot in the middle of the big man's back and pressed down. Nate squirmed but didn't complain.

"Who sent you after me at the Davies' house?"

No answer came. Morgan tromped down hard with his boot heel into Nate's back bringing a howl of pain.

"Who sent you?" Morgan asked.

"Pickering." Nate said.

"How did you know I was at the Davies'?"

"A neighbor saw a man going in and coming out of the back door. She was curious. I . . . I know this lady well."

"Who shot Dunc?"

"Shorty did. He's the man with the two guns."

"And you stripped Faith and tied her on the bed?"

"Yeah, both of us." Nate said.

"You bastard." Morgan pulled his foot off the man. "Roll over on your back." Morgan waited for him to turn over slowly. Then Morgan shot him in the left knee. The heavy .45 slug drilled through his knee cap and exploded the knee joint. Nate curled into a ball, screaming in pain.

"You bastard!" Morgan yelled at him. "It's pay up time. You were with Pickering that night you shot me in the rain, right?"

Nate wailed in his pain. Morgan kicked him in the

side and he uncoiled and lay there sobbing. Morgan repeated the question. Nate wiped his eyes with one hand and looked up through the faint light of the alley.

"Yeah. You should be dead."

Morgan kicked Nate in the crotch, crushing one testicle against his pelvic bones. Nate bellowed in agony for a moment, then passed out. He came to at once, screaming.

Someone started to open the back door of the saloon. Morgan whirled and fired a round into the wall over the top of the door. Whoever it was who was coming out changed his mind.

Nate lay there cringing, trying to hold his knee and his crotch.

"You're scum, Nate. You're the original bastard, do you know that? You probably shot Dunc. You would have raped Faith if you had time. You'll never rape anyone again."

Lee kicked him alongside the head, then again and saw the man's head jolt from side to side. He walked a dozen feet down the alley, then turned and fired two shots into Nate's head.

For a moment a surge of emotion billowed up in Morgan. It was familiar. He had sensed that feeling before. Not pleasant, but not terrible either. It was a combination of power and life and death and doing right and knowing that he had just killed a man and that it was a man who well deserved to die. Then the feeling evaporated.

That's when Morgan knew that he had killed men before, that in the balance he might not be much better than the man he had just killed. At least he had a good reason.

He walked to the end of the alley, almost hoping that Pickering would hear his man had been tricked into the alley. He wanted to be done with Pickering right now and get on with the job so he could learn as soon as possible exactly who he was and all about his regular, normal life.

Once out of the alley, Morgan walked faster. He had to ask Dunc something while he could still answer. Why had Dunc suddenly suggested that they call him Buck until they found out his real name? It wasn't coincidence. Morgan didn't believe in chance. How did he know?

# Chapter Ten

Morgan knocked at the Davies back door. Faith asked who it was, then let him in quickly. He had a grimly satisfied expression and Faith noticed it at once.

"You found him," she said.

"Yes, he won't bother you anymore. You can relax. How is Dunc?"

Her slight frown faded and her mouth opened in silence and then she sobered. She shook her head a moment as if trying to realize that two men were dead. She didn't say anything.

"How is Dunc?" Morgan asked again.

"Oh, he's doing fine. Hasn't got to sleep yet."

"Good, I need to talk to him." He held her hand and they went into the second bedroom where Dunc lay on the pillows, his head up, the light up bright. He was looking at a Ned Buntline Wild West dime novel.

"You got the look of a man who just took care of a problem," Dunc said.

"True. I have another problem. I talked to Mister Lang. He wrote a letter to a guy named Lee Buckskin Morgan. Did you suggest that we call me Buck because you knew who I was?"

Dunc nodded. "In the bureau there, top drawer."

Buck opened the drawer and found the wanted poster.

"I'll be damned. Arizona. Says I killed a man. Sure as hell does look like me."

"I went through the deputy sheriff's stack of wanteds and came up with that one. He hasn't seen it. That stir any memories? Thought better not to say anything about it."

"Just as well. I don't remember a thing about Arizona." He dismissed it. "How are you feeling?"

"Hurts like hell."

Morgan grinned. "Yeah, getting shot tends to do that to a guy. You do what your nurse tells you to. I'm heading out toward the Bibb mine. Mister Lang hired me to get Pickering out of his hair and to see what's going on at the Silver Queen mine. Guess I better get started doing my job."

Dunc nodded, frowned as pain stabbed through him and then took a long, slow breath.

"Yeah, you take care of that. I got that one scattergun right here beside me. Nobody gonna push us around again."

"You're feeling better, Dunc." He pointed at him with his finger and went back to the kitchen.

Faith poured him a cup of coffee.

"You planning on leaving tonight for the mine, or in the morning?"

"Thinking about right now."

"I have a friend, Maxine Garrison. Her husband worked up at the mine. They let him visit her one day every two weeks. She hated it and wanted him to quit. But three weeks ago he didn't come home and hasn't been back since. She might be able to tell you something. I'll write you a note and you can talk to her in the morning. You can't do anything up there tonight anyway."

She put down her coffee and walked to where he still stood near the stove. She pushed hard against him, her breasts crushed on his chest as her lips sought his. The kiss was long and she sighed gently.

"Faith, we can't make love tonight. Not with your father in the house . . . especially since he has that sawed off shotgun!"

She smiled. "I know. I can get a little hugging and kissing, though." She kissed him again and put his hand over her breast.

"A little encouragement, a few dreams," she said. "At least you can play with me a little. I need it after what happened earlier. Right then I thought I'd scream if a man ever touched me again. But now . . . now I want you. So just touch me a little, then I can go to bed happy."

He put his hands inside her blouse and caressed her breasts feeling them get warm and her nipples rise. She spread her legs and pulled one hand down and he rubbed the soft wet spot there through her soft cotton drawers until she shivered. Then he touched the hard node and she climaxed gently against him as they both stood there beside the stove.

Her hand kept his pressed there and he rubbed her again. This time her climax was harder and she moaned in total joy and clung to him. At last she pushed away and rubbed his crotch tenderly.

"Next time big fella, it will be your turn." She grinned at him. "I'm going to say good night to Pa and turn down his lamp. I'll hear him if he even wiggles." She shook her head. "You are more man than I'll ever have again, you know that? Now get to bed before I rip off my clothes and embarrass myself wantonly."

He slept that night on the sofa with a blanket draped over him. The sawed off shotgun was beside one hand and his Colt double action by the other.

The next morning Morgan took a note Faith had written and found the home where Maxine Garrison lived. It was near the edge of town, needed paint and was rundown. He knocked and waited.

He heard a baby cry. A moment later a woman opened the door with a child in her arms. Her hair was carefully combed and she looked scrubbed fresh and clean.

"Morning, I'm Buck Morgan. Faith Davies sent me over to talk about your husband and the Bibb mine. Would you have a minute?"

"About the mine? You hear anything?"

Her face was open, her emotions floating on the surface as the hurt and longing showed through.

"No, ma'am. I'm about to go up there and see what I can find out. Faith said your husband had been gone for three weeks?"

"Come in, come in. I'll put this little punkin' down and we can talk." She turned toward the hallway. "I'll be right back. Sit down."

He sat on a straight chair. The furniture was sparse, and inexpensive. The living room had three wooden chairs, a small table and two pictures on the wall.

She came back and held out her hand. "I'm Maxine Garrison, and Faith is right. Only it's been nearly five weeks now and I'm frantic. I don't know what I'll do. Yes, I'll tell you all I know about the mine."

"I'm not promising I can help. But I'll try."

"He went to work there about three months ago, and then he said that the number of men hired from town was going down. Finally, he said the mine had almost shut down and there were only six of them still there, but that the foreman, Arch Sibling, said they were going to be going full steam in a few days.

"Then Wid went back to work that Monday and I've never seen him again."

"That's all you know?"

"Yes."

She looked up, her brown eyes pleading. Her dark hair was short and neat. For a moment her chin quivered, then her mouth opened and showed white, pretty teeth. Her blouse was open down three buttons and a slice of cleavage showed. She had put on a few pounds after the birth of what must be her first baby.

"Mr. Morgan, you can see how it is here. I don't have any more money. My husband is missing. My baby is hungry. I'm not sure what we're going to eat today. Anything you can do to find out what happened to Wid will just be wonderful. I can do nothing from here.

"I . . . I can't pay you any money, but I want to give you something. I don't know a lot about men, Mr. Morgan, but I do have one thing I can give you. If you wouldn't be offended."

Slowly she unbuttoned her blouse, watching him, waiting for him to tell her to stop. Morgan didn't. He wanted to see her breasts. The buttons came open one by one and her breasts swollen by milk surged out.

"If . . . if you want to, Mr. Morgan, I'll be proud to take you into the bedroom."

The blouse came fully open. She shrugged it off her shoulders and her breasts jiggled, large, taking up half of her chest. They was only a little sag from their bulk and they were milky white with small brown freckles.

She held out her hand. "Mr. Morgan. I believe in paying for services. Since I'm asking you for a favor, the least I can do. . . ."

She stood and caught his hand and he stood.

"You don't have to," Morgan said, his voice hoarse with the urgency of his desire as it surged into fire.

"I understand that, but I want you to be encouraged to look for my husband."

She led him into the bedroom. The baby lay in a crib at one side sleeping. Without a touch of embarrassment she slid down her skirt, then the short underthings she wore until she stood there naked.

Her hips were wide, her belly with a slight rise, and a large triangle of black hair covered her treasure. She walked toward him, hips swaying, breasts bouncing, then she kissed him and held him close. Her tongue went into his mouth at once and she sighed and reached down to his crotch where she rubbed gently.

They didn't say a word after that. She pulled him to the bed and sat him down and undressed him. She frowned at the bandages on his chest, back, arm and leg.

Tenderly she kissed each one, then pulled his mouth to her breasts. They were hot already, burning brightly. He kissed them and nibbled at her nipples until she moaned in pleasure. Then he sucked one breast into his mouth and chewed gently on it. Soon she moaned again and eased backward on the bed flat on her back, open, inviting.

She pulled him with her, her legs spread wide as he lay out over her luscious, hot body.

At once she settled him between her thighs and moved his erection to her wet slot. She looked at him and nodded and he edged forward, then slid into her easily. She made small noises and smiled, then he felt her inside muscles gripping him, relaxing and gripping him again.

Now it was his time to moan in delight and begin his thrusting. She worked with him. He had no thought of his hurts, she was a talented lover, matching his speed and movements, opposing them so it created twice the effect. Quickly he was beyond the point where he could delay. She nodded and he roared into a climax that he wasn't sure he would live through or that he even wanted to. At last he exploded in one last surge and fell on top of her in total exhaustion.

"Wonderful," she said.

He had nearly recovered when he realized she had not climaxed. He pushed his hand between them and found the small hard node and began to rub it.

She looked at him quickly. "Why?" she said.

He kissed her and hit the button again and again. Slowly she began to breathe faster, then her hips began to rotate and in another minute she surged over the top, smashing into a long set of spasms that shook her like a rag in a puppy's jaws and then dropped her. She was limp and spent and her eyes were closed.

"My god! That's the first time!" she breathed.

He kissed her lips softly. "It won't be the last time."

Soon they came apart and he saw a new glow in her face. She looked at him with wonder and awe.

"I've never been able to do that before. No reason. Maybe Wid was not a good lover. I've only made love with two men now, so I don't have a lot of comparisons."

She laughed softly and smiled. "So wonderful! I'm not going to let you leave this house! I'll make a love slave out of you, using you five or six times a day until we both die of exhaustion."

She touched his wounds. "Do they hurt when you get so excited that way, pumping so hard?"

"No, I forget all about them."

"Good. I want you to forget again." She went up on her knees and pushed one of her big breasts into his mouth. "I just love it when you chew on me that way. Can I chew on you? I never have. Wid doesn't want me to."

Her hands went down to find his softness. She played with him and worked and slowly he came hard again. When he did she gave a little cry and pushed him away and eased him down on his back, then knelt at his crotch.

"So beautiful! So big and thick and long and just pulsating. Wid only does it at night with the lights out. I like this way better. You said I could chew on you?"

He nodded. She bent and kissed the purple tip, then down the shaft.

"He's so good, so yummy!" Then she looked at Lee and slowly slipped him into her mouth. He nodded. Her eyes thanked him and she sucked as much of his shaft into her mouth as she could. She made contented noises deep in her throat and then without any urging, she began to ease back and forth on him.

"Oh, god, you don't know what that does to a man," he said softly. He reached down low and found her breasts and rubbed them.

Her lips devoured him, triggered nerve endings he had forgotten about. Slowly he pumped his hips and gradually she held her head still. Then it was time to get serious. He was close to shooting it all.

"Do you want to continue, to let me come?"

She nodded and he felt the first urges, the first closing of valves and opening of channels and the short quick trip of the juice up the tubes.

He wailed and punched harder with his hips, but carefully. She had her hands up now to keep him from spearing all the way through her. His hips bucked again and again and he knew the world had come to an end.

His brain exploded and melted into jelly and his body vaporized and flowed into a crack in the floorboards. Then it all gushed into one huge ball of flames.

She pulled at him after his hips quieted. Then she came away reluctantly and stared up at him.

"I'll never forget you Buck Morgan, not if I live to be 200 years old. Two marvelous experiences. Tremendous."

"The pleasure was mine, Maxine. I'll do everything I can to find your man. I better get ready to go."

They both sat up. He dressed and she watched him. Maxine lounged on the mussed bed, staring. Her breasts hung down and he reached over and petted them.

"The most wonderful, marvelously beautiful part of a woman," he said. Then he kissed both hanging marvels and stood. He put on his gunbelt and cinched it up. He'd left the shotgun and rifle on his saddle.

Maxine got up on her knees on the bed and hugged his chest, pushing her big, soft breasts against his shirt and staring up at him with huge brown eyes.

"I want you to go, but I don't want you to go."

"I have to. I'll look for your husband, I'll demand to know where he is or what happened to him."

He undid her hand and bent and kissed her again, then petted her breasts and she flashed him a big smile that made him want to stay all day and all night.

"Time for one more? It's been a long time for me."

He smiled and shook his head. "I have to find the mine and get ready to go in there tonight. You say there are fences and guards and dogs and everything?"

"Yes, that's what Wid told me." She smiled as she let go of him. "Be careful, Buck. Come tell me what you find when you get back. I'll . . . I'll be waiting for you."

He left quickly then, hurried to his horse and stepped into the saddle. He took the quickest way out of town, then swung around to the north trail that led deeper into the mountains. He'd have the wagon road to follow. Up this valley, across a ridge and into another valley.

Easy. Earlier he had saddled his horse in the livery and paid for another week's stay, then went out the back gate so nobody would see his horse leaving. Now was not the time to take a chance for Pickering to spot him. He'd deal with Pickering later.

Right now, he had a mine to find, he had to earn a thousand dollars, and he had to discover some secret that Mister Bibb plainly did not want found out.

# Chapter Eleven

The first five miles went quickly as he cantered the horse and then walked her. They made good time. He wanted to get to the mine area so he could slip up on it and observe it, recon the place before it got dark.

Recon? That was military. Had he been in the Civil War? With a start he realized he didn't even know how old he was. That would come in time, he decided. It plagued him that he had lost his memory. So he probably was this Buckskin Morgan. Who the hell was that?

Was he really wanted in Arizona for murder? If he was an outlaw there, he might also be a wanted man in maybe half a dozen other states, including California. Damnit to hell! He wished he knew all about himself!

He rode harder then, and eased off when he figured he had covered about nine miles. He was into the second valley. Far ahead he could see smoke, smell it now too. Smell it? He must be something of an outdoorsman. A hick from Chicago would not be able to smell smoke out here from ten feet.

He moved up to corners in the wagon road cautiously now. He had met no one, nor seen a soul since he left Silverville. What was going on up here anyway?

At the next corner he could see the mill ahead. A collection of unpainted buildings. He could make out the hoist house, the two mine entrance tunnels, a larger place where the ore must be broken down and refined somehow, and a big stamping mill. He scowled. So he knew what they were, he couldn't remember how or why he knew. Maybe he was a hard rock miner.

He backed around the corner and rode into the woods. Silverville was about five-thousand feet in elevation. He had been steadily on an upgrade since he left the small town and figured he was around the seven-thousand foot level here. Lots of trees, pines and firs and lots of brush from the winter rains and snow pack. He would have no trouble riding almost up to the mine through the cover.

When he spotted it, he had been about half-a-mile away from the mine. He rode another quarter-of-a-mile north, located a patch of dense brush and worked into it. Soon he found a small clearing where he could picket the horse. Nobody would find it unless they charged right into that spot. It would make a good hidden camping spot if he had to stay over the night. He had matches for starting a camp fire if he needed them. Always come prepared was his policy.

Morgan left the shotgun hidden behind a tree, took his borrowed Remmington single shot rifle and began working his way uphill through the brush toward the mine.

It took him half-an-hour. He moved like an Indian, slowly, not making a leaf rustle or a branch creak. He faded from one tree to the next, and soon could look out on the Silver Queen mine from fifty yards. A well made eight-foot-high barbed wire fence was less than twenty feet in front of him.

The fence was carefully built with the barbed wire strands no more than four inches apart on posts set every ten feet. The fence was hung with tin cans that would rattle and clatter if anyone tried to climb it and probably if anyone even touched or bumped it.

On top of the fence a two foot extension came down at a 45 degree angle to the inside. This, too, was layered with barbed wire. The fence looked like one he had seen at a prison once. Bibb didn't want anyone to get out of his mine location. Now just why was that?

Morgan lay there concealed by brush and tall grass and watched the mine. The layout was about what he expected. A small building with windows that was obviously the mine office. He figured it had living quarters in the back. The stamping mill clattered as iron struck iron mashing the ore into small pieces so the chemicals could go to work extracting the silver and any traces of gold that was in the silver bearing quartz.

The smelting operation building was just down from the stampers. He saw men moving around. Set back from the other buildings, up the little creek that ran down through the mine enclosure, were two buildings that looked like dormitories. If the miners stayed up here, the management would have to furnish them a place to eat and sleep.

The mine entrance tunnels were both busy, with

men pushing out cars loaded with ore. Once it hit daylight, the car was hitched to a pair of mules and it was pulled toward the stamping mills, working up a slight incline so the ore could be dropped into the stamping chambers.

Nothing out of the ordinary so far. How did he know that? Had he been a miner? From that distance, he couldn't see the men who pushed out the ore cars plainly, but they looked small. Why? Were small men an advantage in mining so the tunnels could be smaller?

It was past midday. He wondered if the men had been fed a meal? Probably they got two meals a day so they could stay underground at midday. Were there shafts in there that dropped deep into the mountain, or were the tunnels directly to the rich vein on this same level? He could see no ventilation shafts up the side of the mountain. But if there were no shafts, why would they need a hoisting shack and mechanism?

He was working up too many questions.

Five men pushed an ore car out of the tunnel, helped get the mules hitched and an outside man drove the mules up the incline. One of the men from the mine slipped away to the side behind a pile of tailings and stretched out. The other four men from the car went back into the mine, evidently to push out another car of ore.

Now Morgan saw the guards. There were three men walking the fence. All had rifles. The closer one came toward him on this section of the fence, the clearer it became. He carried a Spencer repeating carbine. It could fire eight shots of .52 caliber without reloading.

That was a mighty good and expensive weapon for a guard to be carrying. He checked the man hiding in the slag heap. Twice he had rolled over to keep out of sight of the patrolling guards. When the two guards on the part of the fence nearest to the slag pile were at the farthest point from the man hiding, he began crawling toward the fence.

Morgan lifted his rifle to help the man, but at once he knew he could not fire a single shot. If he did there would be guards out through the gate hunting him. He could lose them in this brush and get away. But that would not be helping out anyone like this man who evidently was being held here against his will. Why else the guards, and fences?

The escapee had made it halfway to the fence. The guards turned now and started the boring job of retracing their steps.

Suddenly the man trying to get away must have realized he was running out of time. He lifted and ran for the fence twenty yards away. He got there without being seen, then used a pair of wire cutters and broke one of the wires about waist high. The snapping wire and the clanging of the tin cans set up a reaction around the whole fence.

The guards checked their sectors quickly and a cry went up from the man just to Morgan's right.

"I see the bastard!" the man called. His rifle came up and he fired twice, missing both times. The man trying to escape cut two more wires and lunged through the fence. He got only halfway through, then the barbed wire caught on his ragged pants. He tried to pull them free.

Three rifles snarled almost at once and two of the rounds hit the runner, jolting him against the fence. He struggled again and surged against the wire, falling half on the outside. Two more shots slammed into his body, then it hung on the fence, motionless and lifeless.

Morgan turned away. He could have helped the man! Sure, and he could have been shot himself. He wanted to earn his $1,000 and report back, not get himself killed.

The guards blew whistles and three more men ran out of a guard shack with rifles ready. They talked with the head guard and then the three new men hurried away and came back with wire splicing and tightening equipment. They pushed the body of the dead man out through the hole and left him there. Then they quickly repaired the spot and put on one extra strand of barbed wire just to make sure.

The men worked about thirty yards from where Morgan lay concealed in the brush. The three looked like anyone else, 20 to 30 years old, white, wearing suntan pants and shirt, evidently a kind of guard's uniform.

At the far side of the complex, he saw smoke come out of a smaller building he guessed was a cook shack. He checked his watch. Nearly three in the afternoon. He wondered how the food was, but decided he couldn't break in and then get in line for chow call.

Powder shack? Where would they keep the dynamite? Any good mine had lots of the new dynamite and caps and fuses around for rough tunnel faces. He looked over the entire place again and found a wooden door over a dugout to the far right next to the fence. Looked like a safe place. They must have dug a hole and put logs over the top and a slant door. If the goods blew up they wouldn't blast down every building at the mine.

Morgan watched. He saw a few more guards as they changed places. The mules were behind now as a dozen small ore cars had been pushed out to be dumped into the stamping mill crushers. They might build up a surplus so the stampers could work all night.

Morgan dozed. He snapped his eyes open and looked around. No one was near him. He had no idea how long he had been sleeping. His watch showed that it was after five o'clock. Then he saw what had awakened him.

A line of men came out of one of the mine tunnels. They were chained together with ankle irons on their right ankles. They marched in a long row. None of these men wore shirts, only grimy pants and shoes. He tried to count them. Over forty of them.

They walked with their heads down. A rifleman guard led the way and marched them to the barracks at the far end of the camp.

*Slave labor!* No wonder no one had returned from this place. He was too far away to get a good look at the men, but somehow they all seemed to be small. All were smaller than the guards. But the guards might all be six-feet four.

There was no doubt now. He had to go into this place. He had to free those prisoners. So it wasn't his job. This kind of inhuman shit he wouldn't stand for.

Morgan pulled back from the fence and worked his way through the brush uphill toward where he had seen the powder magazine. He found it again and edged up as close as he could get to the fence. The trees were all cut down inside the fence, but they hadn't bothered with those outside. He found a pair of young pine trees growing close together.

He could use them to get inside. Once inside getting out would be no problem. But first he needed the shotgun. He took the rifle and ran downhill through the brush. He was confident now that they had no outside sentries or scouts. They figured they were safe inside their barbed wire!

He found his horse and moved her closer to the bottom of the fencing, then took the shotgun and his supply of shells. Good thing he had remembered to pick up a box of the double-ought buck rounds. Now he moved them into his pants pockets front and back and his shirt pockets. When he needed them he would want them fast. He left the rifle on the horse. It was a daylight sharpshooter's weapon. Tonight he needed the scattergun and all the rounds he could pump out.

He jogged back up the hill and got there just before the sun slid behind the far mountain top. He saw the cooks in the cook shack take food to the building he figured was the headquarters. Then they used a wheelbarrow and took large pots up the hill to the barracks. These men were not going to have a gourmet supper.

Morgan memorized the layout of exactly where the buildings were. Everything depended on there being a good supply of dynamite in the powder bunker. If it turned out the place was a potato cellar, he was in lots of trouble.

But at this place he figured the management would be more likely to have more dynamite than potatoes.

An hour later it was totally dark. He checked on the twin pine trees he had seen. They grew six feet from the fence and were about 30 feet tall. Buck tied the shotgun around his back with a stout rawhide thong, then began climbing the pine trees.

Within seconds his hands were covered with sticky pitch from the pines, but that would help him hang on. He got above the fence and kept climbing.

When he was ten feet over the fence he tested one of the young pines by swinging out to the side toward the fence. It bent gracefully to the side, then held.

Morgan climbed another ten feet until the trunk of the pine was less than an inch in diameter and stretching only six feet over his head. He would need only one of the pines. This time when he leaned to the side, the tree bent to the left toward the fence. He grabbed the trunk with both hands and swung outward, pushing away from the bending trunk with his feet.

The added weight on the top of the tree bent it smoothly to the side. He cleared the fence by six feet and just before the bending branches of the pine touched the top strand of the eight foot high barbed wire fence, he let go. His feet were only four feet from the ground. He landed easily and kept his feet.

The pine made a swishing sound as it straightened into its previous position.

Morgan grinned. He was inside and he had left no evidence of his entry for a fence walking guard to spot.

# Chapter Twelve

Morgan ran to the wooden door leading underground and checked it in the soft moonlight. He could see no warning wires or safety devices. There was a padlock on the hasp over the door but one smash from the butt of his Colt and the lock popped open. He swung one of the doors up and saw steps going down. He went in until he was shielded from the outside, then he struck a match.

Yes. The powder magazine. There were at least twenty cases of dynamite there. He lit another match and found boxes of dynamite caps and rolls and rolls of fuse.

Morgan figured he could set a lot of charges in ten minutes, so he cut off 20 ten-foot lengths of fuse, making them all the same length, doing it by feel. When he had those ready he set them on the ground outside of the bunker and then lifted out three 50-stick boxes of dynamite. They were packed in sawdust so they wouldn't jostle against each other and explode.

Morgan struck another match in the bunker and

picked out ten dynamite caps and put them in his one pocket without any shotgun shells. He just hoped that they didn't bang together too hard, or he would be the next explosive item to be heard from.

Outside, he closed the bunker door and pushed the padlock back in place, pressing it together so it looked to be locked.

Then he moved cautiously toward the buildings and settled down to wait. He had to spot where the night guards were. They wouldn't need fence guards since the workers were all locked in ankle chains.

Ten minutes later he saw one guard leaning against the hoisting house. He was smoking a cigarette and gave himself away by the glowing ember on the end.

The second guard coughed. He was just outside the mine office building. After another half hour, Morgan could find no more guards. These two should go off duty about midnight, he figured. He could wait. He had work to do.

First he lifted the wooden tops of the boxes and took out dynamite. He carried an armload of 18 sticks and took six lengths of fuse and went to the fence across the bottom of the compound farthest from the office building. He wedged three sticks of powder under the wires on the first post just at the ground level.

Then he made a hole in the soft dynamite with a stick, and pushed in the dynamite cap. Next, he pushed the end of the ten-foot long fuse in the hollow end of the cap and it was ready. Then he went to the next post. He mined six posts in a row and hurried back to his dynamite.

He would light the fuses later.

Just to be safe, he carried all the dynamite, fuses and detonators a hundred feet from the powder magazine to a little spot of brush. Then he began to plant bombs everywhere that the guards would not spot him. He put ten sticks at the entrance to the mine, another on the back of the cook shack. One more fused bomb went under the back side of the mine office.

The mine office deserved the most, a half case of dynamite—25 sticks. He set a fuse into the whole batch. What a bang that was going to be! It would be the first blast to go.

He moved cautiously up to the back side of the hoisting building and set a ten-stick package under it. All the bombs so far had ten minute fuses. He hoped this fuse was normal and burned at the rate of a foot a minute.

Next, he circled the barracks. He watched them for ten minutes, but could find no guards. Without a sound, he slipped into the back porch and tested the door. It was locked. From his pocket he took a piece of stiff wire he had brought with him, bent it, and a moment later had the simple skeleton key lock open.

He stepped inside and listened. Men sleeping. A few muttered in their sleep. He risked a match and checked. Single bunks and the men were chained to the bunks. The locks on the leg irons were good ones. He couldn't open them. He'd need a key. One of the guards would have one in case of fire. He checked one sleeping man again with a match near his face.

He was Chinese. Morgan used another match and checked two more faces. Chinese. No wonder the men had looked small.

He slipped out the door and faded into the night

to a spot where he could watch the two exterior guards.

He looked up at the moon, then at the north star. The pointer stars on the big dipper were angled up at the north star as if they were coming from the '8' on a watch. That made it almost midnight. He had no idea how he knew that.

Five minutes later, a shaft of yellow light streamed from the mine office building and a door slammed. Two figures walked into the night, and a few minutes later the two guards were relieved and went back into the office building with the fresh ones taking over.

Now he would eliminate one of the two guards, then get the prisoners released.

Morgan worked up through the darkness to where he could see the two guards. He found the first one at the same place next to the mine office. It took him some time to locate the second one near the hoist shed. This one positioned himself around the corner, just out of sight of the mine office building guard. So much the better.

Morgan circled, came up behind the hoist shed and then began to edge around the wall. He moved like an Apache, no noise, no sudden changes in shadow patterns. He pulled out his boot knife and crept forward.

Now he was at the corner and could see the guard leaning back against the wall, his automatic rifle hanging over his shoulder by a sling. His hands came up to his face to light a cigarette.

With the flare of the match, Morgan drove forward. He ran only eight feet away. The match blinded the guard for a moment. In that half a second, Morgan slammed into the man, drove his six-inch knife deeply into the guard's side and ripped it out to the front.

He felt the blade reach the ribs and grate off them, then ease outward and the guard dropped limply from his grasp. Morgan caught the rifle before it clattered to the ground. The guard slumped face down into the mountain dust.

Morgan took a deep breath, bent and worked through the guard's pockets. He would have to keep a key in case of some disaster so the slaves could be freed during the night. Morgan found the key in the dead man's second pocket. He slipped it out. It was a long thin rodlike affair, more like a wrench.

He pushed it into his pocket, took the rifle and hurried away toward the barracks with the hoist shack shielding him from the other guard.

In the barracks with the door already open, he slapped the first Chinese man gently. He awoke with a start.

"English?" he asked softly. "Do you speak English?"

The man blinked, shook his head, but pointed across the aisle at the second bunk.

Morgan shook that Chinese awake and asked the same question.

"A little," he answered.

"I have the key to release all of you. You're going free tonight. I want you to wake each of the men and tell them all to be quiet. Not a sound. Understand?"

"Yes."

"Are there men in the other barracks?"

"Yes, Mexicans, about thirty. Also a few white men."

"I'll unlock these men, you come along and tell them to be quiet."

Morgan hurried down one aisle and up the other

unlocking the hated leg irons. He warned the man again to keep everyone quiet until the explosions, then they should run to the fence and when the shooting stopped, they could go through the fence and away.

Morgan ran to the second barracks. He unlocked the same simple door lock and was inside.

At once he found the white men. He told them what was happening and they told the Mexicans. Five minutes later he had the thirty men free. Then he asked if Wid Garrison was there.

"That's me," one man said.

"Come with me," he said. "You ever use a rifle?"

"Yes, sir."

They ran to the fence and Morgan found a place for him where he would have a field of fire covering the office building.

"How many guards and bosses?"

"Twelve guards and four others."

"Wid, you ever killed a man before?"

"No, but I damn well can kill any of those sixteen right now!"

"Good. I'm going to start lighting the fuses. First I'll get the mine office, then the other buildings. Last, I'll come down and light the fuses for the fence. I should be able to get them all before the first one goes off.

"Remember, if the Chinese or the other prisoners forget and come charging through here, don't shoot at them."

Morgan ran into the night. He got in back of the big mine office building and lit the fuse, then ran to the hoist shack and the cook shack lighting both there. He continued to the entrance to the mine and lit the fuse there, then on down to the fence.

"Hey, Willy," the guard at the front of the mine

office building called softly to the second guard.

Willy couldn't answer.

The guard tried it again. "Damn, Willy. You sleeping again on duty gonna get your ass whipped."

Still no response.

"Hell with you. Ain't my ass."

Morgan continued on to the fence and lit the fuse. Each of the six fuses here was low enough in some weeds so it wouldn't be seen by the guard. He lit the last one, then sprinted for the spot where Wid Garrison crouched.

"Damn soon now this place is going to blow up," Morgan said. "I talked to your wife in town. Faith Davies told me to ask her about this place. I'm working for the other guys. When I saw those damn leg irons and chains, I got a little mad."

Garrison blinked tears out of his eyes. "I was about ready to give up and die. We lose one man a day up here. I don't know where he gets the Chinese and the Mexicans."

Just then there was a brilliant flash and the rear twenty feet of the forty foot long mine office lifted off the ground and disintegrated, showering half the mine camp with bits of lumber and roofing.

The guard standing in front of the building was knocked flat. He struggled to his feet. Wid aimed at him and fired twice. The guard screamed and jolted to the ground.

Two men ran bellowing in fear from the front of the bulding. Morgan stood and slammed a round from the shotgun at them, then realized he was too far away with the scatter effect of the cut off barrels.

He ran forward, came within twenty yards and fired again, blowing both of them four feet backwards into hell.

Glass broke on the far side of the building and someone jumped out. Two shadowy figures rushed away into the darkness.

Just then the cook shack exploded and a moment later the hoisting building.

When that explosion died down, the ten sticks of dynamite blew up at the mine entrance.

Morgan ran around the shattered office building looking for any survivors. He found one, a guard evidently who had his arm blown off. He lifted his hand for help, then slumped to the ground, dead of shock and loss of blood.

Morgan fired twice into the broken windows, then heard the string of explosions obliterating a fifty foot length of fence.

That sound died away and Morgan looked at the barracks.

"Now, Chinaman friend," he bellowed. "Get your people out of here."

He heard chattering along the far fence, then saw shadows slipping down the side of the enclosure to where the smoking remains of the fence lay flat on the ground.

The Mexicans and six white men came down along the fence a moment later. Morgan saw no new targets. He ran back to where he had left Wid Garrison. He and another man were crying on each other's shoulders.

"My friend," Garrison said to Morgan. "We kept each other alive these three weeks."

"You might as well go with the rest of them, Garrison. I've got a little clean up to do when it gets light. Nothing else much is going to happen here tonight.

"Try to make as little noise as possible. I'm watching for a pair that got away. Who lived up front in the building nearest the front door?"

"That would be the mine general manager," Garrison said. "He's a real geek named Mr. Hyde. An Englishman who is a sadistic bastard."

"The foreman lived up there, too," Garrison's friend said. "I still think that Englishman likes little boys. Damned if I don't."

"Might have been the pair who survived the blast and got out a window," Morgan said. "I'll be watching for them right here until daylight."

Garrison shook Morgan's hand, as did his friend. Then they stepped gleefully over the blasted down fence and hurried out to the road.

Morgan moved to the midpoint between the gap in the fence and the gate. If one of the survivors was Mr. Hyde, he would have a key to the gate. Now was no time to be sloppy.

Buck waited the rest of the night. Near daylight he heard someone moving toward him. Just as it grew light enough to see more than twenty yards, two men with partly burned clothing came away from the fence on the far side and headed toward the gate.

One of the men seemed misshapen with one shoulder higher than the other. He walked with a limp. The man behind him held a pistol and kept searching the area around him.

Morgan took the Spencer and made sure there was a round in the chamber, then lifted the rifle and put one round through the pistol waver's heart.

At the sound of the shot and the sudden death of his friend, Mr. Hyde held up his hands.

"Don't shoot, old boy. I surrender. I don't know where you all are, but there must be half an army of you. I give up. I capitulate, for god's sake."

"Walk over this way," Morgan said. Hyde knew where he was by then from the small cloud of blue smoke from the .52 caliber Spencer round. "Easy does it, or you're as dead as the rest of your slave mongers."

"Slaves? Certainly not. These men all worked for wages."

"Sure, Hyde, sure. And you're the Prince of Wales." Morgan had tied the shotgun over his back, and held the Spencer loosely. He had not used his six-gun.

"Let's take a tour of the office and see what's left, Mr. Hyde. You first."

"You did a jolly good job of bashing it in. Found our dynamite, did you?" He looked around. "Where are the rest of them?"

"Aiming their rifles at you at this moment from just beyond the fence. A security force. We weren't sure how many guards you had up here."

"I daresay not enough."

He led the way to the office and stepped inside through the door knocked off one hinge.

Morgan slung the Spencer carbine and drew his Colt.

"Don't grab a weapon, or any tricks, Mister Hyde. If that happens I start shooting you in the elbow, then the knees and work up toward your black heart."

Hyde nodded and opened a door marked "private." Inside, the window had shattered inward from the twisting of the frame building. A large desk had not moved. Pictures on the wall had fallen.

"The cash box," Morgan said. "And open the safe. I'm taking over as official administrator of this mine as of today. So dig out all of the valuables, now."

"I hardly think that's fair," Hyde said.

Buck brough the Colt down across Hyde's forehead, slamming him to the floor, tearing two gashes across his head that dripped blood down his face.

"Do it, now!" Morgan said, his voice steady and edged with a deadly steel that Hyde reacted to automatically.

He opened a locked drawer to his desk and took out a metal box. He lifted the lid to reveal stacks of greenbacks. He went to a picture hung low on the wall and pushed it aside. Behind it was a wall safe that extended into a closet.

Inside was a heavy bank cash bag, nearly full. Hyde pulled it out and nearly dropped it. It took both hands to lift it to the desk top.

"Gold double eagles," he said. "Then there are the pure silver bars ready to be shipped to the mint in San Francisco. There are ten of them, each weighing ten pounds."

"Where?"

"In the safe."

"How many men have died at this mine since you've worked it, Hyde?"

"What? I really don't know. I didn't keep records."

"One a day?"

"No, not that many. One a week perhaps in the past two months."

"I heard it's one a day, that's sixty. How many died on the wire trying to escape?"

"What? Oh, three or four, we warned them."

"So you and your men here killed sixty-five men, and worked the rest half to death as slaves. That's highly illegal, even for a fine talking Englishman like you."

"I'm ready to face the court," Hyde said.

Morgan had what he wanted.

He turned to one side and let his gun drop down a ways. Hyde reacted better and quicker than Morgan expected. He kicked the gun out of Morgan's hand, pushed him over the desk and darted out the door. Morgan picked up his gun and walked to the broken window. Hyde came racing out the door heading for the blown down fence.

Morgan fired twice. Both rounds hit the man in the back, the first smashing his spinal cord, the second jolting through one shoulder. He died before he crumpled into the dirt.

"Yes, Mr. Lang, I'll be able to give you a complete report on what is going on at the Silver Queen mine," Morgan said.

# Chapter Thirteen

Morgan stared through the window at the man lying on the ground. Was he dead? Hyde was the sneaky kind who just might play possum. He went out through the broken door and turned Hyde over with his foot. There was no breath, no pulse at his wrist.

Good. As Morgan stood, a sudden wave of dizziness hit him. It sometimes did when he stood up too quickly. Only this time it was worse. He put out one hand to steady himself, then knew he was falling. His hands went out but then he passed out and slammed into the ground hard, his forehead bouncing off the packed dirt.

Morgan came to slowly, shook his head to clear it and tried not to move. If he didn't move they might think he was dead. Then he realized that it wasn't raining. In fact, he wasn't even wet.

"What the hell?" Morgan said and sat up. His head spun again but then settled down and he looked around where he sat. This wasn't a street. He'd been in a shootout with five or six guys and ran out of rounds, then he got kicked about a thousand times.

He looked around at the mine.

"Oh, damn. I came to this town to work for Janish Lang."

He looked down at the body in front of him and memories of the past few days came flooding back.

He remembered it all; Faith and Dunc, him getting shot, the shootout in the alley and the guys with the shotguns. Then he talked to Lang and came up to the Bibb mine.

"The slaves!" How could anyone do that to human beings? He got up and remembered what Hyde had showed him inside. He hadn't even looked at the money. Just how much was it worth to a man to be shot and stomped and nearly killed?

A hundred-thousand dollars? Maybe not that much. He checked the weapon at his side. His own Colt Double Action. It felt good having it there. Automatically, he replaced the fired rounds from the piece and holstered it.

In the office, he looked at the cash box. They were twenty and fifty dollar bills. He had no idea how much cash was there. The sack of gold double eagles was real. Maybe two hundred of them. An ounce each that would be about 13, 14 pounds. He hefted the sack. More like 20 pounds. Three hundred and twenty double eagles. That would be more than $6,000.

"Yeah, we're getting there," Morgan said. He looked in the safe and saw the silver bars. There weren't ten of them, there were twenty. He rubbed his jaw. Gold was worth $20.67 an ounce, set by law. Silver, best he could remember, was about $1.30 an ounce. So a pound would be worth about $20. The silver bars were worth about $200 each.

Not worth carrying around. He took two of them for Dunc to use in his jewelry business. Morgan decided the money he had found would about settle his financial account with the shooters. He closed the safe door and twirled the dial, then carried the goods out the front door. He found his horse right where he left it.

Morgan put the two silver bars in one saddlebag and the stacks of greenbacks and the double eagles in the other one. Then he took the borrowed rifle and the shotgun and headed back down the trail toward town.

He expected all of the walkers would be in town or beyond by now, all ready to get as far away from Silverville as they could.

It took him about three hours to make the ride to town. He went slowly, trying to think through the whole thing.

Two loose ends. Bibb and Pickering. Pickering first, the bastard. Pickering shot him when he was down and helpless. Evening up time was due. Now he remembered it all. Pickering would not have a side-shooter to soften up his target this time the way he did with that shootout in the street.

Morgan rode right up to the back door at Dunc Davies' house and tied his horse. Before he could get the saddlebags off, Faith came running out the kitchen door.

"Thank God!" She threw her arms around him and kissed him.

"Inside, woman. You want to ruin your reputation?"

She grinned. "I don't care. You're back!"

He tugged the saddlebags off the horse and put them over his shoulder, then shooed Faith inside. Once there, with the door closed, he hugged her properly and kissed her.

"How is Dunc?"

"He's feeling better. Doc was by this morning, early. Said he looks good and that there isn't any infection, yet. We're hoping."

Faith tapped her toe on the floor. "Well, tell me. What happened out at the mine?"

"I found your friend's husband. He should be home by now. Bibb was running that place with slave labor. The only way you quit was to die. Let's go in and I'll tell both you and Dunc at the same time."

He went through it all. Right down to getting his memory back.

"So now I remember everything." He looked up at Faith who was standing above Dunc. She reddened a little. He went on. "I know why I came here, who I am. Everything. And I've about figured out how much I'm charging Bibb for having me gunned down."

Dunc grinned. "How much?"

Buck showed them the gold and the bills and the two silver bars. "This much, however much it is." He picked up the two silver bars. "These aren't worth hauling around. Only worth about $200 each. Thought you might like to have some silver to use in your jewelry business. Melt it down, make rings, things like that."

Dunc grinned. "I've done a few things. Silver comes in handy." He frowned for a minute. "Don't worry, I'll be sure to get rid of the mine imprint on that bar. Thanks."

"Oh, that also pays up my board and room for another two days. Speaking of board and room, I could use something to eat."

"You haven't had a thing to eat since breakfast

yesterday!" Faith said frowning. She ran toward the kitchen.

Morgan took out the stacks of greenbacks and found them already sorted into the various denominations. He counted the bunches and Dunc wrote down the amounts. When they were through they had a total of $3,485.00.

Morgan looked up at the watchmaker. "Dunc, if you had your druthers, what would it be? Looks like this town'll be lucky to have silver for another year or two. What then?"

"I always have liked Sacramento. Been there before. Give a good bit to have a shop downtown, do watch repair, sell some fine timepieces and a whole passel of clocks. Course, have some rings and stones and jewelry things."

"Sounds like a good future there," Morgan said and stood. "I better get washed up and oil my Colt and put the long guns away. That little shotgun is a dandy. You rest up now and we'll have you back to work in a week."

Morgan held out his hand. "Thanks for saving my skin back there. I'd have been dead for sure if you and Faith hadn't come and hauled me out of that muddy street."

Dunc snorted. "Don't mention it. Do the same for a stray dog if'n he was hurting." Dunc said it, then grinned and blinked to keep the wetness from seeping over the sides of his eyelids.

Morgan ate two meals, had three cups of coffee and sat in the sun out in the backyard for an hour. Then he went inside and touched Faith's shoulder and she turned around and hugged him.

"Now that you remember everything, you're probably riding away. I mean, you came here on a job. You do it and leave, right?"

"Right, usually. Sometimes I get lazy and stay awhile."

"You look real lazy to me," Faith said. She kissed him hotly. Then pulled back and whispered in his ear. "I want you in my bed so much that I can hardly stand not ripping your clothes off right now."

Morgan grinned and kissed her quickly. "You just keep your knees together for another day or so and we'll see what we can do about taking care of those wild, sexy desires of yours.

"I have two personal items of business first." He held up the stacks of greenbacks. "Oh, do you have a safe place where you can put this."

"Sure. How much is there?"

He told her.

"Probably more cash than the Silverville bank has right now. I'll put it away."

He kissed her forehead and took the long duster coat from the coat closet and put it on. Under it he slung the double-barreled shotgun and fastened the top two buttons. The big gun was entirely hidden. He waved at Faith and walked out the back door. The shotgun might come in handy. He had six extra shells still in his pockets. He rode straight to the Hard Rock Cafe and walked inside. The barkeep looked up and started to make a signal when Morgan stopped him.

"Pickering in the back room?" Morgan demanded, his tone had that deadly, no nonsense edge on it.

"Yeah. Alone."

Morgan pushed around the bar, checked behind him, and then went through the door quickly, his six-gun up covering whatever was ahead. It was a short hall with one door open to a storeroom. The other door was closed.

He unlatched the knob, then kicked the door inward.

Pickering sat at a table, pouring a shot of whiskey into a drinking glass.

"Don't even drop the bottle," Morgan said. "Pickering, you don't have five guns backing you up this time."

"Don't need them. I don't work for Mr. Bibb anymore."

"You're forgetting me, back shooter. I want a large piece of your skinny hide full of double-ought buck holes. You and me, right now. We're walking out the back door to the alley. Move it, now!"

"What good that do you?"

"I won't get your blood all over this fine room. Out!"

They walked down the hallway, with Morgan protecting his back all the time. At the alley door, Pickering stepped out, then slammed the door toward Buck and took off on a run. Morgan stopped the door with his boot and rammed it outward.

His first .45 shot hit the running Pickering in one of his long legs and he crashed into the dirt and rolled twice. He came up on one knee.

"Now, now!" Pickering screamed.

Two men in the alley fired revolvers at Morgan. Both were behind trash bins or burn barrels. He had no cover. He took two steps and dove for a large wooden box. One slug grazed his right shoulder before he got behind the cover.

He fired once more around the box, catching Pickering as he hopped toward the sturdy protection of the saloon's outhouse. The round nailed Pickering in his other leg and flopped him into the dirt.

Morgan pulled up the shotgun and when one of the back up men tried to run to another safe shield, Morgan fired. The 15 .32 caliber sized balls slashed through the air in a widening circle. By the time they got 30 feet to the running man, seven of them jolted into his flesh.

Two hit him in the side, two more in his neck and three in the side of his head. He spun to the left, hit the dirt and rolled three times, then dropped through the gates of hell.

The second gunman who must have been there to protect Pickering, crouched where he had moved to behind a large cardboard box. Morgan snorted at the protection. He pushed a new round into the ten gauge and then fired into the top of the box.

The slugs lifted it and blasted it over the crouching man's head. The second round from the scattergun pulverized the gunman before he recovered from the shock of being a wide open target. The .32 caliber balls drove him backward into the side of the furniture store and he died screaming.

Pickering held up his hand. "I got two shot up legs, I don't have a weapon. Get me to a doctor and I'll tell you all you want to know about Bibb. He's your next target, right?"

"Start talking," Morgan said, remaining behind his cover.

"Damn, you hold all the cards. Yeah, you're right. He used slave labor. Got most of the Chinks from Sacramento and San Francisco. Promised to pay them two dollars a day. All they got was cold rice and chicken soup until he worked them to death. The Mexicans he brought up from down south somewhere. Same deal. Two dollars a day. He never paid them a cent."

"He live in his office on Main?"

"Right. He's got two sawed off shotgun guards in the front of the place, one in back. Also a big black goon who can't talk but who can break a man in half with his hands. Does what he's told to do."

"What's this Bibb character like?"

"You've never seen him? He weighs about 400 pounds. Eats eight meals a day. Has a chef he brought from San Francisco. Likes little Chinese girls, I mean young ones, 12 or 13. I've never seen him walk. The big Nigra wheels him around in a chair that becomes his bed. That's about it."

"The cook live in?"

"Yeah, but you call him a cook and he'll scalp you."

"Anything else?"

"About it. The guards work 24 hours a day. They take turns at night."

"All right, Pickering, you earned it easy. Get up and walk."

"Walk? I'm shot in both legs."

"So they aren't broken, walk. Your choice, walk out of the alley or die where you sit."

Pickering whimpered with pain as he stood, then walked slowly down the alley. It was three blocks to the side of the mountain where the houses ended. They went another two blocks beyond the houses and Pickering stopped.

Morgan walked up within six feet of the man and glared at him.

"How many men you shot in the back when they're helpless, Pickering?"

He didn't answer. "Go ahead, get it over with. You didn't make me walk out here for my health."

"You haven't suffered enough. Your men shot Dunc Davies. The old man never even met you."

Morgan shot him in the right shoulder, high up where the .45 slug rammed into the joint and turned Pickering into a blubbering hulk.

"Finish me!" Pickering screamed.

Morgan didn't say a word. He watched the man. "At least I know that you'll never mash up another man and then shoot him in the back."

"Get it over with!"

Morgan lifted the reloaded shotgun and pulled both triggers at once. The thirty .32 caliber balls from the two rounds tore off Tim Pickering's head and sent it rolling down the slope for 20 feet.

Morgan turned around and walked back to town.

His next stop was Janish Lang. It was nearly three o'clock when Morgan knocked on the front door of the house where the mine owner lived. A woman said her husband was still at the mine. Morgan was welcome to go out and talk to him there. She gave him directions.

Fifteen minutes later Buck stepped up to the building that had a sign which read, "Big Strike Mine Number One." He pushed open the door and went inside.

Two men worked at desks and one of them looked up.

"I'd like to see Mr. Lang," Morgan said.

The clerk went to a closed in office, knocked and went in. A moment later he was back and nodded.

Morgan went into the room and shook hands with Lang. It was a stark, undecorated office.

"Is it true, the stories I've been hearing around town about the Silver Queen?"

"What stories, Mr. Lang?"

"About the slave labor mostly. I've heard there were over 50 men working up there in leg irons."

"That must be true then, Mr. Lang. I'm afraid the

mine is out of operation right now. Seems there were several explosions up there. The guards and the foreman and the mine general manager must have been caught in the blast."

Lang sat down and scowled. "I didn't mean for you to kill anyone up there, Morgan. I just wanted a report."

"I'm giving you a report. Everything else up there that happened was on my own. They were killing one man a day, working them to death. I saw them shoot down a man trying to get through the eight foot high barbed wire fence. The guards and bosses up there weren't men, they were animals. That was my good deed for the day."

"Pickering?"

"He won't bother you or any of your men anymore."

"I suppose you killed him, too."

"I just know he won't bother your men."

Lang rubbed his face. "Now I'm sorry I brought you in here. You're worse than they were. I'll have this on my conscience for a long time."

"While you think about it, think of Wid Garrison. Wid was one of the white slaves. He'd been up there for months. He said since they started the slave operation, they have killed over 60 workers. Murdered them. Worked them to death," Morgan said.

He looked at the miner. "You're a good man, Lang. But good men don't clean up nests of rattlesnakes like Bibb brought in here. It takes a specialist. I was the man you needed. I did the job. Now, I'm here to collect my wages."

"Yes, yes. I'll pay you. Then I hope you get out of town."

"That seems to be my business, Mr. Lang. By the

way, you need another good miner—I'd suggest you contact Wid Garrison."

Lang nodded. He counted out ten one hundred dollar bills from an envelope he had prepared and handed it to Morgan.

He rubbed his face again with his right hand. "Sorry I said all those things. You did what I asked you to do. I was just . . . I was at the end of my rope. I didn't know what to do."

"I got my memory back, Mr. Lang. At least I know for sure who I am now. I can live with that." He turned and walked out of the room.

Morgan rode his horse to the back door at the Davies house and tied her. He hurt as he eased out of the saddle to the ground. He hadn't hurt this much for two days. Most of the tension was gone, the nervous energy that kept the pain beaten down had evaporated with the life of Pickering.

Now all the pains surged back in his chest and back and leg. He got to the kitchen and met Faith. He held up his hand. She had to help him get out of the long duster.

Then he dropped in the chair. Faith brought a whiskey bottle and a glass and sat them on the table in front of him.

He nodded, tossed down a shot and coughed. He shook his head and drank the next one slower.

Faith sat close to him. "You don't really like the killing, do you?"

"Not always. But sometimes when I see vicious, terrible men causing others suffering and pain and death, then I don't mind at all evening up the score for the ones those men had killed. Pickering was just as bad as the others. He was twice removed from the actual scene."

"Is it over?"

"Almost. I have nothing to do until midnight."

She caught his hands and brought them to her breasts. He gently pulled them away and kissed her.

"No, I have to stay angry. I'll take a ride. I'll eat supper if you cook something, and I'll kiss you goodbye like I might never come back, which I might not. Then if I do, I'll be done with it, paid off and finished, and we'll make love all night and decide what to do tomorrow."

"Do you have to go out? Couldn't you just call it off now and stay here? Why take a risk of being killed again?"

"Don't argue with me. This is the way it has to be, that it must be. The odds are that some day, I simply won't come back. I never figured that I'd live forever. I don't know if I've made a mark, left the world any different than when I came into it.

"But this is the way it has to be. I can't let the biggest villain of all get off free to dirty up another town somewhere. I can't let him ride away unscathed."

"We can get the law on him," Faith said.

"Not likely. That would take a month. By then he'd be in Colorado or Alaska or Montana looking for another sucker game to play on people."

"Kiss me once more and I'll cook you supper."

He kissed her, not feeling good about it. But she seemed satisfied and went back to the roast she was cooking on top of the stove.

"I'll be back in an hour," he said. He went out the door and rode into the light timber south of town. There he took out his Colt and did some target practice. He put thirty rounds through his weapon, some off a fast draw, some firing six rounds as quickly as he could pull the trigger.

When he was satisfied, he went back to the house

and tied up his horse. Inside the meal was ready. They both took trays in and ate with Dunc. He appreciated it.

Dunc looked at Morgan. "You got another bone in your gullet?"

"One more, Dunc. One more damned big bone to fix, then I'll be able to breathe easy. I'll be back late tonight—if I can make it back."

"Oh, damn!" Dunc said, and stared at Morgan with sad eyes. He knew it was going to be a tough job.

# Chapter Fourteen

Two hours later, Morgan was at his observation point. He had climbed the fire ladder in back of the two story hardware store and walked to the front where he had an ideal view of the one story building across the street with the Silver Queen Mine sign on it.

Lights glowed in the front office until just after nine o'clock. Then they went out. Morgan thought of burning out the fat man, but if he did and the fire got away, it would also burn down half the town.

The wooden buildings were built one against the other one, sometimes having a common wall. The torch plan was out. Smoke bomb so they could think the place was on fire? No, one of his guards would find such a device and throw it into the street or the alley.

He had to do it the hard way. The big bastard who ordered the slave labor was not going to get off free. He was the one who had put the gunmen on Lee Buckskin Morgan, and Morgan wasn't going to put up with that going unanswered.

By now Bibb must know what happened out at the mine. He couldn't ride out and take a look. Not without a carriage and two horses. Then he'd have to get into the carriage.

Bibb might have sent someone out to check it for him by now.

What other options did he have for getting to the fat man? There were no openings on the roof. Other business firms pushed up against each side protecting it. Defending the place would be simple. One shotgun guard in front and one in back.

So he had to eliminate one of the guards. How? A woman, a fire, a dog, a shotgun blast, a knife. Yes. It had to be a knife, quick and silent. Face to face with blood spurting into his face. The kind of killing that takes guts.

Dynamite!

He thought about it. He could put a two stick bomb on the front door and the back door, time the fuses to blow at almost the same time, then dash inside during the confusion. Maybe. He climbed down from the roof and walked past the front door of the mine office. He checked the minute and second hand of his watch.

Then he ran to the closest end of the block and down to the opening of the alley behind the mine office until he got to the back door. He checked his watch again. It had taken him 43 seconds to make the run. He could set the rear fuse a minute faster than the front one. Three minutes on the front, two on the rear.

Yes, he'd try it.

He went to the hardware store's back door. It was solid with a bar across the door from the feel of it. The windows on the first floor had bars on them.

The second story windows did not. He stared at them for a minute, then looked around the loading dock. He found what he wanted, a stack of 50 gallon water barrels. There were six of them. The window was 12 feet off the dock. He stacked up three of the barrels and the top of the third one extended up almost ten feet.

Morgan put another barrel next to the stack of three and stood on that one. Then he climbed to the top of the third one and reached the window. It was locked with a turn device. Morgan used the side of his fist and broke the foot square pane of glass without cutting himself.

He reached inside and unlocked the double hung window and slid it upward. He crawled through. He was in the second story storage room.

Below in the back room he found the underground vault where the dynamite was stored. The top had only a half-inch iron lid on it and no lock. He lifted it and found an opened box of dynamite. He took out four sticks, then thought a minute and took out two more. He found fuse and caps close by in another box. One piece of fuse he cut off at three feet, another at two feet. He then cut four more pieces four-inches long.

In his shirt pocket he put six of the thin copper blasting caps, the detonators. In the front of the store he took a sack and scratched out three handfuls of roofing nails, inch long with large round heads. He found some tape and put a roll in his pocket. Then he put everything back the way it had been and checked the back door. It had a bar on it.

He went back out the way he had come in and closed the window and locked it. Only the broken pane would show tomorrow. He took the barrels down and placed them as they had been and faded

into the darkness down the alley. He sat there on
the ground and taped the two-stick bombs together.
He used a pencil stub to punch a hole in the powder
and inserted the dynamite cap into the hole. Then
he took the other two sticks of dynamite and cut
them in half with his knife.

Around each of these half sticks he taped thirty
of the roofing nails. When the powder exploded the
nails would be blasted out in a deadly spray, cutting
down anyone in the way.

He rigged four of them with the detonator
imbedded in the stick ready to receive the fuse. The
four-inch fuses should burn for fifteen seconds.
That was time enough for a safety edge, yet not
enough time for someone to find the bomb, grab it
and throw it back at him—he hoped.

The last thing he did was push the proper length
of fuse into each of the hollow ends of the dynamite
caps. Then with his explosives all ready, he found
a place to watch the alley window of the fat man's
place and waited.

Someone blew out the lamp just after midnight.
Morgan moved at once. He walked around to the
front of the building and wedged the two-stick
bomb in the fancy handle on the front door. He saw
no one on the street.

A saloon a block down erupted with three men
staggering out and shouting, but they moved in the
other direction. Buck shielded a match and lit the
three minute fuse. He ran then, moving quickly
down to the end of the block and down to the alley
and hurried up to the fat man's back door. There
he pushed the second two-stick bomb against the
base of the heavy door and lit the two minute fuse.

Morgan pulled back from the sputtering fuse and
ran fifty feet down the alley and slid in behind a

large wooden packing box. He didn't want to light a match to check the time. Slowly he counted down the rest of the two minutes.

He was at 57 on the second minute when he heard the blast at the front door that rocked the little town and probably blew out a window or two. He had just nodded his head when the blast just down the alley lit up the space for a moment, then the billowing roar of the two sticks came and a shock wave that slapped at the box and swept on past. He heard pieces of wood falling and stood and looked at the back door. He brought up the double barreled shotgun and raced for the spot where the rear door once stood.

Now it was a shattered mass of kindling, only small sections near the hinges remained. Some of the door had been blasted inside the room smashing into a wall. A form ran into the void holding a long weapon.

Morgan brought up the scattergun and triggered one round. He was close enough now. The double-ought buck smashed into the rear door guard, jamming him backward against the wall where he hung for a moment, then the big slugs jolted on through his body ending his earthly experiences forever.

Morgan darted through the smashed door and saw a light still burning down a long hallway. A form came out of a room on the left. He wore white pants and screamed in some foreign language. French? He ran toward Morgan. It was obvious he was scared to death and not a danger. Morgan let him charge past him and then he saw another figure down near the lamp. This one held a shotgun. Morgan dropped to the floor just before the weapon went off.

Even as he fell, Morgan triggered the second barrel of his own scattergun. He heard the other man's pellets slanting over his head, drilling the space where he had been with death dealing lead. His own round was fired from a low angle, coming upward. Two of the .32 caliber sized shot caught the shooter under the chin and ripped his head upward. Four more hit his chest, jolting through ribs and into his heart and chest, dumping him in the hallway, another dead piece of meat.

There were two more protectors to worry about, Morgan thought as he stayed where he was. He reloaded his shotgun and checked the handgun in its leather. It was still in place.

The hallway was deathly still.

A noise came from the front somewhere. Then all was still. He heard a team and rig somewhere in the front, through the blown off front door perhaps, out on the street.

Nothing moved.

Morgan got to his knees, then to his feet. Something was not right. There should be some movement.

He heard wheels rolling, squeaking. Pickering had said the fat man was wheeled around by the big black man.

He was leaving! Morgan surged down the hallway. His foot hit a wire across the hall and he slammed quickly to the floor as a shotgun blast boomed just over his head. Three or four of the spreading pattern buckshot bounced off his shirt and kept going. The weapon had been tied to a chair in a room to the left and aimed gut high.

Lucky. He had been damn lucky. He heard the team out front again and more squeaking of wheels. Morgan moved forward, watching the doorways now. There were three more between him and a larger opening near the front.

There still had to be the third shotgun guard somewhere and the big black. Where were they?

He checked the next room, empty. As he peered into the hall from the floor level, he spotted a face moving back from the doorway to the next room.

The door was open. Morgan pulled out one of the half sticks of dynamite from his pocket and lit the four-inch fuse. He held it as it burned halfway down, then flipped it into the room across the hall where he had seen the face.

Six seconds later the half stick went off, sending out thirty roofing nails like large pieces of shrapnel. The explosion seemed greater inside the building. Dust and smoke billowed from the room followed by a scream and then a frothy, bubbling sound, then silence.

Morgan jumped to the doorway and looked in through the dust and smoke. A man lay crumpled against the blown out window's frame, his body studded with the roofing nails, a dazed, surprised expression on his dead face.

Ahead, he heard reins slap on the backs of horses. Morgan ran through the rest of the offices, through a kitchen and a bedroom, then the outer office with its blasted in doorways. He caught sight of a carriage weaving down the street as it raced south out of town and toward the Sacramento road.

That had to be Mr. Bibb getting away. Furiously, Morgan raced back inside and checked each room he hadn't been through. There was no one else there. He ran outside and down a half block to a saloon. Three horses stood outside with reins around hitching posts and their heads down, sleeping.

He picked the one with the broadest chest and pulled the reins. Morgan vaulted into the saddle and jerked the just waking up horse around and aimed him down the street. Bibb and his carriage couldn't get far. Morgan had only the shotgun and his pistol. No long range work this time.

He charged forward, galloping the surprised beast for two blocks, then stopped dead still. He could hear a rig ahead of him still south on the stage road.

Morgan let the mare settle down to a mile eating canter and worked along the blackness of the night road. It was easy to follow with the help of light from a half moon. A carriage even with two horses couldn't go fast very long.

He relaxed in the saddle, counted the double-ought buck rounds he had left, six, and made sure his gun was in place. Now all he had to do was ride them down.

When he was sure the mare was well warmed up, he put her into a moderate gallop again. This time, as the trail led up a small rise, he could see the carriage ahead. The horses were walking up the hill. Morgan kicked the animal with his heels and it raced ahead.

He nearly got there before the rig reached the top but it went over the rise and just before it went down the other side a wink of light showed and a booming sound of a hand gun drifted back to him. He was still a hundred yards away, five times out of the range of the weapon.

Morgan pushed his mount faster up the hill and paused briefly at the top searching the rig below. Then he spotted it racing down the incline too fast. He watched as the carriage swung to the far side of the road, ran two wheels in the shallow ditch a moment, then came up and went to the other side where the front wheels hit something and the whole carraige tipped up on one side, then rolled over, breaking some of the traces and knocking down one of the horses dragging the rig.

The whole thing came to a sudden stop and the downed horse screamed with what must be a broken leg.

Morgan rode down slowly, the shotgun across his saddle, his finger on the trigger.

Someone moved below, and before Morgan got to him, the big man limped off into the night. A Negro. He was gone and out of it. He wasn't about to get killed for the fat man.

Morgan remembered the hand gun and when he was within twenty yards of the wreck, he got off, tied his horse and sat on the ground watching. Nothing moved for five minutes. Then the horse screamed again.

A pistol shot exploded shattering the stillness. The horse lifted its head, then rolled over and died.

"I hate to see an animal suffer," a voice said from the upside down carriage.

There was a silence again, then the fat man broke it. "You gonna sit there all night or come help me get out of this tangle?"

Morgan laughed. "Figure you aren't going anywhere. I can wait until daylight and make sure you don't have the six-gun anymore."

"You must be this Lee Buckskin Morgan I keep hearing about."

"The same."

"You ruined my mine," Bibb said.

"And set free your fifty slaves," Morgan replied.

"And killed my four managers, twelve guards."

"They knew the risks they were taking when they

signed on."

"This is getting us nowhere. Mr. Morgan, you're an intelligent man. Also good with dynamite and that shotgun. I propose a truce. Let's talk about a bargain that will make you a rich man."

"We've got all night to talk."

"Look at it this way. I made some money here, I gambled going after too much, too soon, and I lose. So I cash in my chips and move on to another situation. I have money in Sacramento. You get me safely to Sacramento, and I sign over the Silver Queen to you, lock, stock and silver bars. The whole thing is yours."

"Is that all? I hear the Queen is about worked out. That your ounce per ton figure is way down. You're dealing a stacked deck, Bibb."

"Not at all! The vein is getting wider all the time. We have two veins, with a potential of a million dollars. You go in with some capital and hire good men and it can be making money in a month. Then you sit back and get rich."

"How can I get you to Sacramento? I hear you don't sit a horse none too good."

A chuckle came from the wreckage. "True. I tend to weigh down one horse. All I need is another carriage and driver to get me to Sacramento. We're only about fifty miles from that town. You can go back to Silverville, hire a carriage and horses and meet me here in an hour. I'll work my way out of this tangle. I'm not helpless. Then we ride to the capitol."

"What's my guarantee?"

"I'll put it in writing. I always have pen and paper with me, a failing of mine. A travel kit. That's where I got the pistol. Derringer, in fact. I'll write out the bill of sale, giving you total rights to the mining claim, the mine, the below and above ground buildings and all equipment, and any silver still on site. It will be a legal and absolutely unbreakable bill of sale for the sum of one dollar."

"Sounds legal enough. How do I know you won't tear it up before I get back."

"Oh, I'm an honest man, Mr. Morgan. I honor my guarantees, stand behind my word."

"Rather have a little more assurance than that. You write out the bill of sale. And throw out the pistol where I can find it. Then when I have it, you fold up the bill of sale and push it out through the carriage there."

"All of this isn't necessary. . . ."

"It is if you want to get to Sacramento," Buck snapped. "When I see that the paper is written, I'll go back aways and light some matches and read it. Then will be time enough to go back for a carriage."

There was a long silence, then a big sigh. "All right, all right! I hate to bargain. I'll write out the bill of sale now. I, too, will have to burn some matches so I'll have light to write by. I trust you won't shoot me as I'm making you a rich man."

"Never do that, Mr. Bibb. No sir. I've never been rich. I been poor. I hear rich is better."

"Indeed it is, Mr. Morgan. Do you see my light? Even now I'm writing out a legal bill of sale."

Morgan waited. He could see the light now past part of the torn top. He had all night.

It was ten minutes or more and a lot of burned matches before the call came.

"There, I'm done. All legal, proper and in an envelope. I signed and dated it. You saw where my light was. You work up toward me there and I'll throw out the derringer. When you're satisfied that you have it, I'll put a rock in the envelope and pitch out the bill of sale.

"You have me at a serious disadvantage here. There is not a chance I'll hurt you. You're my one lifeline to get to Sacramento."

"Yeah, I think you're right," Morgan said. He kept low and crawled toward the spot he had seen the light. In the pale moonlight he saw an arm come out and throw something. It hit a rock and bounced toward Morgan.

A minute or two later he had the derringer. It had been fired both times and the spent rounds were in place.

"Fine, Bibb. Now throw out the bill of sale."

The arm came out again and threw a white item. It sailed and landed closer. Morgan waited, then found a stick and pushed and dragged the envelope toward him. He lay in a slight depression offering him cover. He still didn't trust the man, even though he had never seen him.

Morgan took the envelope and crawled away, got behind solid protection and opened the sealed flap. He read the letter. It was in a fine hand in ink, dated and signed. He was no lawyer but it looked legal to him. He folded it and put it in his pocket.

"I read it, Bibb. It looks legal. How is that other horse down there? I haven't heard anything from it."

"Poor creature died in the crash, broken neck I'm afraid."

"A shame. Too bad your black man wasn't a better driver."

"He was frightened of the animals. I told him to slow down. He's powerful with his hands, not with his head."

"A little more about you, Bibb. I'd guess that you've milked a few good mines before this way?

Almost like highgrading it?"

"Goodness, yes. I'm a specialist. I move in, buy up a good mine, take out the best ore as fast as I can and then sell it off while it's still somewhat profitable. The sucker who buys it thinks he's got a rich one."

"Why the slaves?"

"Profit, my good man. Profit. Why pay a miner a dollar a day when I can get one for free? That's an extra thouand dollars a month in profit."

"But you worked them to death. Didn't that defeat your purpose?"

"Depended on the time schedule. I had another two more months of good highgrading here. Then I'd be gone. All we had to do was keep the secret for two more months. That was Pickering's job. But thanks to you he failed miserably."

"I've got a surprise for you, Bibb."

"I like surprises. What is it?"

"You'll see in a minute."

Morgan had moved bck up to within 30 feet of the wreck. Now he took out one of the half stick of dynamite nail bombs and lit the fuse. He threw it as soon as it was burning. The device landed just short of the buggy wreckage and ten seconds later it exploded with an ear splitting roar since the dynamite was resting in the open.

"What the hell?" Bibb thundered when the noise had died down. "You're supposed to go get me a carriage só we can drive to Sacramento."

"Sorry, Bibb, never trust a gunman."

"You promised!"

"Not really. If I did, I lied. You can sue me," Morgan said. "I keep thinking about those fifty or sixty men who died in your mine."

"They weren't *men*. They were Chinese and Mexicans," Bibb said.

"Men in my way of thinking."

Morgan lit the second bomb and threw it. It dropped through a hole in the side curtain of the smashed carriage and exploded within four feet of the 400 pound man.

The roofing nails blasted into his bulk, but only one did any damage, that lanched into his neck but missed a vital artery or vein.

He bellowed in fear and anger. "Stop this! I made you a rich man."

"In a highgraded worked out mine?"

Morgan threw the last bomb. It went on the other side and fell behind the seat partially deflecting the explosion. Two of the roofing nails blasted into Sylvester Bibb's face. One thundered through his left eye and into his brain. The second hit point first and drove an inch and a half into his forehead.

After the last blast, Morgan heard nothing from the wrecked carriage.

He waited an hour, dozing now and then. When he thought it was safe, he lit a torch of some heavy grass and weeds that had turned brown, and went up to check. He found Sylvester Bibb dead and growing cold on the rear seat of the wrecked carriage.

A leather carrying case four inches thick and a foot and a half square was clutched in his arms.

Buck tore the case free and carried it back to his horse. He was less than three miles from Silverville. Buck rode the distance slowly, letting the animal walk. In town, he tied the mount at a different saloon than where he had found him. Then Lee Buckskin Morgan walked back to the Davies' house, the shotgun in one hand, the leather case in the other.

He'd look and see what was in the case tomorrow. Yeah, tomorrow would be plenty of time.

# Chapter Fifteen

It was almost four A.M. when Morgan came to the Davies house. There was still a light on in the kitchen. He tried the door and found it locked. He knocked.

A moment later the door opened and a revolver barrel poked out.

"Who is it?"

"Lee Morgan."

"Oh glory!" Faith rushed into his arms before he could get inside and close the door. "You're still alive. We heard about explosions and shootings and gunfights, all sorts of wild things going on tonight." She touched his face tenderly, then kissed him hard on the mouth.

"Oh, first, Pa turned bad, and two men took him over to the Doc's house on a door. Doc says he's got a touch of relapse, and he wanted to keep him there in his sick room for a day or two so he can watch him all careful. But he says not to worry. Pa will be fine."

She kissed Morgan again and pushed hard against his body with hers. "Now tell me what happened. I been waiting up for you. Went to sleep with my head on the table for a spell."

He told her as she heated up some coffee. She watched him wide-eyed, then stared at the bill of sale.

"It ain't legal, is it?"

"Far as I know. Looks right. I'll show it to a lawyer tomorrow if there's one in town."

"Good! Now you'll be staying here and I can have you every night! You got a silver mine to run!"

"Not likely. First we find out if the bill of sale will hold up, then we see if there's any silver ore still in the mine. Then will be time to decide what to do with it."

He looked at the case on the table. His cut arm had broken loose again, he knew. He could feel the wet blood inside his shirt.

Morgan took the case and tried to open it. There was a small lock and a place for a key. He shrugged and reached in his boot for the long knife and cut the leather flap in half. He spread the sides of the case and looked in. Stacks of greenbacks. The outside showed hundred dollar bills. He fished out some envelopes that looked like they held grant deeds to property.

There were half a dozen railroad stock bearer bonds that were unnamed and good as cash.

"Looks like Bibb was running out of town with all the money in his bank account." Morgan's eyes slid closed and he nodded.

"Time for bed for you," Faith said. "We'll count everything in the morning."

"My arm," he said. She took off his light jacket

and shirt and scowled.

"You hurt it again."

"I'm still alive, that's what counts most."

She put the salve on it, then wrapped it up with some more of the strips of sheets she had torn.

Faith took him to her bed and helped him undress, then he dropped on the sheets and never moved.

"Tomorrow you're not going to get off so easy," she said.

She kissed his lips gently, then undressed and snuggled down naked beside him pushing back until she touched him. Then she slept as well.

Faith was up at seven with a fire going and ready to make breakfasst whenever Buck woke up. At last she went in and sat beside him awhile, then she peeled the light covers back and kissed his lips gently. He mumbled. She kissed him again, then slipped into the bed beside him.

Her hand found his crotch and caressed him and stroked him. Quickly he was hard. Faith took his hand and put it on her breasts. Automatically he began to fondle them. He smiled in his sleep. She moved his other hand down to her own crotch and he grinned and opened one eye.

"Am I being seduced?" he asked softly.

Faith jumped. "How long have you been awake?"

"Since the first time you kissed me. I've been enjoying it."

She hit him with a pillow, then slid back beside him. "Why don't you continue?"

He did, setting her on fire, burning her into a white hot coal and then a white ash that drifted away on a light breeze. She opened her eyes and knew that she didn't ever want to move again. She would simply stay here on her back with him inside her and resting gently on top of her with her arms clasped firmly around his back.

"Hey," he said softly.

She opened her eyes and the spell was broken, but this one was almost as good.

"Yes, beautiful man. Yes, best lover in the world. Yes, I'm here and loving a man I love and not afraid to say it."

"We have work to do. First breakfast, and then the lawyer, and then see the Garrisons. I have a job for him."

"What kind of a job?" she asked.

"Not sure yet, depends on what the lawyer says."

"Dunc says I have to to go the shop today and stay open from ten to five so people who left watches to be repaired can get the ones that are ready. We better hurry."

She made a quick breakfast, then they dressed and Morgan realized that he had worn the same clothes ever since he came to town. He had arrived with no duffel. Today he'd buy some new clothes.

First thing would be the clothes, he decided. He settled for a new shirt and a brown leather vest and a hat, low crowned and brown. No red diamonds on the head band, but he'd watch for one of those.

The only lawyer in town was named Oliver Bowden. He looked at the bill of sale for a long time and turned it over.

"From what I can see it looks legitimate enough. All the required items are there, the intent, the compensation, the signature, the date, the location and complete description of what is being sold. Yes, if I'm representing you, Mr. Morgan, I'll work hard to make anyone prove that this is *not* a legitimate bill of sale."

"Fine, you're my new lawyer." He gave the man a twenty dollar bill for the consultation and another hundred dollar bill for a month's retainer. Oliver Bowden almost collapsed from surprise.

"Dear me, this does seem to be an excellent situation," Bowden said. "Just call on me when you rename the mine and set up your operation."

Buck called at the bank and discovered that Mr. Bibb had closed out both of his accounts the previous day just after noon.

His next stop was to see Janish Lang in his mine office. He showed Lang the bill of sale, and Lang looked up surprised.

"I don't understand."

"He's been highgrading the mine. Tearing out the best veins he can find, working everyone to death, and then ready to dump the property while it still looks valuable but is a shell. We stopped him well before that time."

"How did you ever get him to sell the mine, and for nothing more than a dollar?"

"He wanted me to take him to Sacramento."

"Oh." Lang looked up, confused. "And did you?"

"No. Mr. Bibb suffered a fatal injury when his Negro attendant drove a carriage down the first hill out of town and lost control. The rig crashed, killing one horse and breaking the other's leg. It was destroyed. Mr. Bibb wanted me to come back to town, get another carriage and horses and drive him to Sacramento where he had funds, he said.

"After he wrote out the bill of sale his injuries proved to be fatal."

"And you had nothing to do with that?"

"I wasn't driving the rig, no sir."

Lang took a deep breath. "Things change so rapidly around this business."

"I want you to make an inspection with me of the Silver Queen, see if she's worth saving and working."

"Why me?"

"Because I can trust you, and because I want you to be a fifty-fifty partner in the operation. You know mines, I don't. You can run a mine, I can't. I would suggest we leave as soon as possible and take along Wid Garrison, who was one of the slaves working in the mine and should know it well.

"If this all works out, it would be my suggestion to hire Mr. Garrison as the general manager of the Silver Queen."

"I don't know. I'd be in competition with myself."

"Not at all. It would be a logical expansion for your operation."

"I hear most of the buildings were wrecked. Take a lot of money to put it right again."

"True. I'm ready to put up five thousand dollars in cash. With another five thousand from you, that should be enough capital to get the operation going and into production."

"Damn, you've thought of everything."

"I try, Mr. Lang, I try."

They took a buggy and stopped by at the Garrison house. Wid was sitting on the steps whittling. He recognized Lang and stood up and brushed off his pants. Then he saw Morgan and raced out to meet him.

"Wid, good to see you again," Morgan said.

Wid grabbed his hand and pumped it. "Never was

so glad to see a mortal being in my life as when you slipped into them barracks up there."

"Wid, we want you to come back up to the Silver Queen. Me and Mr. Lang here are the new owners of the mine. Want you to show us around, see if it's worth getting back into operation. What's your first evaluation?"

"Oh, hell yes. There's lots of good ore in there. They had us grabbing only the widest veins. From what I've seen, a normal work day up there should last for at least three years just on the veins we know about now. Plenty of ore in there, yes sir."

"Good, grab your hat and let's take a buggy ride," Morgan said.

When they came back well after dark, the deal was consummated. Lang's own company lawyer drew up the partnership papers and they signed them. The bill of sale and the new deed would be signed over at the county seat as soon as they both could get over there. The next day work crews would go in to begin tearing down the buildings and putting up new ones, salvaging what they could.

The hoist house never had been used. They should be back in operation within a week. Wid Garrison had accepted the job as construction foreman and when the mine went into operation, he would handle the job as mine foreman, and general manager.

Later that night at the Davies house, Morgan and Faith counted the money in the leather case. The stacks of bills totaled $8,600. Bonds worth another $5,000 were in the case.

"The man did not go around without some

funds," Morgan said. He looked at the stacks of bills. "I had a talk with Dunc. He'd like to move to Sacramento and open a store there. I want you to be sure he does it."

She shook her head. "He's happy here. Why move? Besides, it costs a lot."

"No worry there. You haven't been paid for saving my life. Dunc might not take it, but I know you will."

"Take what?"

"Remember that cash I asked you to put away somewhere?"

"Yes. It still scares me to have it in the house. It's $3,485.

"Right. That and another $1,515, makes it an even $5,000. That's what I'm paying you for saving my life. I know, I know . . . it's not very much, but I'm a cheap guy."

"You . . . you can't do this. Dunc would never take it. I mean, all we did was what anyone. . . ."

He kissed her. "You take the cash or I'll never kiss you again."

She laughed softly and kissed him. "I'll take it, but Dunc is going to have a cow fit, I mean, an absolute heifer of a stomping around."

"I'll tell him while he's still sick. Oh, we have another job, to count those gold coins. I need $5,000 worth to set up the Silver King mine."

They counted the double eagles. There were 324 of them, for a total of $6,480. They put $5,000 worth in the canvas bank bag and pushed the rest to one side.

Faith was awed by all the money.

"I've never seen so much money in all my life. Do I have to think that it's stolen?"

DOUBLE ACTION • 167

"Absolutely not! This money is in payment by Mr. Sylvester Bibb for compensation to me for his almost killing me. The price is low. I should have charged him more.

"Now, if you don't have any more questions, let's get all this filthy money put away somewhere. Then let's eat something and then see if that bed of yours is big enough for two before we go see Dunc. He should be ready to come home today."

"And then you'll be talking about leaving, won't you, Lee Buckskin Morgan?" A tear slid down her cheek.

"A time comes when I'm due to move on. But not for a week or so. Have to get the new mine started, and check out the work force, and get Dunc well enough to move to Sacramento. That's going to be interesting telling him about it.

"I can put that off a while. We'll figure out what to do with the money later. Most of it will go into the bank. And I'll send a bank draft to my bank in Denver. If I have any left I might buy you a pretty new dress."

"Right now I don't want to think about dresses," Faith said as she pulled him into her bedroom and let her dress drop to the floor. "I'd rather think about not having a dress on, or anything else for that matter."

Morgan chuckled. It was great to have his memory back. It was so fine to have a beautiful, eager young woman undressing in front of him. And it was pleasing to think about what would be coming when he moved on down the road. He'd been thinking about San Diego lately. No reason. Might be time he went down there again and checked out his former friends.

"Hey, you're miles away," Faith said. She had pulled off the rest of her clothes. "Seems like I'm always undressing you."

Lee Buckskin Morgan grinned and kissed her. "Yeah, I like it that way."